KU-018-916

A Beautiful Wedding

ALSO BY JAMIE McGUIRE

Beautiful Disaster

Walking Disaster

Red Hill

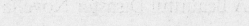

A Beautiful Wedding

A Beautiful Disaster Novella

JAMIE McGUIRE

**SIMON &
SCHUSTER**

London · New York · Sydney · Toronto · New Delhi

A CBS COMPANY

First published in Great Britain in 2013 by Simon & Schuster UK Ltd
A CBS COMPANY

Copyright © 2013 by Jamie McGuire

This book is copyright under the Berne Convention.
No reproduction without permission.
All rights reserved.

The right of Jamie McGuire to be identified as author
of this work has been asserted by her in accordance with sections
77 and 78 of the Copyright, Designs and Patents Act, 1988.

1 3 5 7 9 10 8 6 4 2

Simon & Schuster UK Ltd
1st Floor
Gray's Inn Road
London WC1X 8HB

www.simonandschuster.co.uk

Simon & Schuster Australia, Sydney
Simon & Schuster India, New Delhi

A CIP catalogue record for this book
is available from the British Library

ISBN: 978-1-47113-356-5
eBook ISBN: 978-1-47113-357-2

This book is a work of fiction. Names, characters,
places and incidents are either a product of the author's imagination
or are used fictitiously. Any resemblance to actual people living or dead,
events or locales is entirely coincidental.

Printed and bound by CPI Group (UK) Ltd, Croydon, CR0 4YY

For Deana and Selena

If I was drowning you would part the sea
And risk your own life to rescue me . . .

—FROM JON BON JOVI, "THANK YOU FOR LOVING ME"

A Beautiful Wedding

CHAPTER ONE

Alibi

Abby

I could feel it coming: a growing, persistent unease that crept just beneath my skin. The more I tried to ignore it, the more unbearable it became: an itch that needed to be scratched, a scream bubbling to the surface. My father said that the urgent need to run when things were about to go wrong was a like a tic, a defense mechanism inherent in the Abernathys. I'd felt it moments before the fire, and I was feeling it now.

Sitting in Travis's bedroom, just hours after the fire, my heart raced and my muscles twitched. My gut pulled me toward the door. Told me to leave; to get away, anywhere but here. But for the first time in my life, I didn't want to go alone. I could barely focus on that voice I loved so much describing how afraid he was of losing me, and how he was close to escaping when he ran in the opposite direction, toward me. So many people died, some of them strangers from State but some were people I'd seen in the cafeteria, in class, at other fights.

We somehow survived and were sitting alone in his apartment, trying to process it all. Feeling afraid, feeling guilty . . . about those who died, and that we had lived. My lungs felt like they were full of cobwebs and flames, and I couldn't get the rancid smell of charred skin out of my nose. It was overpowering, and even though I'd taken a shower, it was still there, mixed in with the mint and lavender scent of the soap I used to scrub it away. Equally unforgettable were the sounds. The sirens, the wailing, the worried and panicked chatter, and the screams of people arriving on the scene to discover that a friend was still inside. Everyone looked the same, covered in soot, with identical expressions of bewilderment and despair. It was a nightmare.

Despite my struggle to focus, I did hear him say this: "The only thing I'm afraid of is a life without you, Pigeon."

We had been too lucky. Even in a dark corner of Vegas, being attacked by Benny's goons, we somehow still had the advantage. Travis was invincible. But being a part of the Circle, and helping to organize a fight in unsafe conditions that resulted in the deaths of countless college kids . . . that was a fight not even Travis Maddox could win. Our relationship had withstood so many things, but Travis was in real danger of going to prison. Even if he didn't know it yet, it was the one obstacle that could keep us apart. The one obstacle that we had no control over.

"Then you have nothing to be afraid of," I said. "We're forever."

He sighed, and then pressed his lips against my hair. I didn't think it was possible to feel so much for one person. He had protected me. It was my turn to protect him.

"This is it," he said.

"What?"

"I knew the second I met you that there was something about you I needed. Turns out it wasn't something about you at all. It was just you."

My insides melted. I loved him. I loved him, and I had to do whatever I could to keep him safe. Whatever it took—no matter how crazy. All I had to do was talk him into it.

I leaned against him, pressing my cheek against his chest. "It's us, Trav. Nothing makes sense unless we're together. Have you noticed that?"

"Noticed? I've been telling you that all year! It's official. Bimbos, fights, leaving, Parker, Vegas . . . even fires. Our relationship can withstand anything."

"Vegas?" I asked.

In that moment, the most insane plan formed in my mind, but the idea made sense as I stared into his warm, brown eyes. Those eyes made everything make sense. His face and neck were still covered in soot mixed with sweat, a reminder of how close we had come to losing everything.

My mind was racing. We would only need necessities

and we could be out the door in five minutes. We could buy clothes there. The sooner we left the better. No one would believe two people would get on a plane right after such an enormous tragedy. It didn't make sense, which was exactly why we had to do it.

I had to take Travis far enough away, for a specific reason. Something believable, even if it was crazy. Luckily, crazy wasn't that far a leap for Travis and me, and it was possible the investigators would second-guess the dozens of witnesses who saw Travis fighting in the basement of Keaton Hall that night—if they had proof that we were in Vegas hours later getting married. It was absolutely insane, but I didn't know what else to do. I didn't have time to come up with a better plan. We should already be gone.

Travis was staring back at me expectantly, waiting to unconditionally accept whatever came out of my crazy mouth. Goddammit, I couldn't lose him now, not after everything we'd fought through to get to this moment. By anyone's standards, we were too young to get married, too unpredictable. How many times had we hurt one another along the way, screamed at each other one minute and fallen into bed together the next? But we'd just seen how fragile life was. Who knew when the end would come along and sweep one of us away? I looked at him, resolute. He was mine, and I was his. If I knew anything at all, it was that only those two things mattered.

He furrowed his brow. "Yeah?"

"Have you thought about going back?"

His eyebrows shot up. "I don't think that's a good idea for me."

Weeks ago, I'd broken his heart. Travis chasing America's car when he realized it was over was still fresh in my mind. He was going to fight for Benny in Vegas, and I wouldn't go back there. Not even for him. He had gone through hell while we were apart. He'd begged me back on his knees, and I was so set on never returning to my life in Nevada, I'd walked away. I'd be a complete asshole if I asked him to go back. I half expected him to tell me to get the hell out for even mentioning it, but this was the only plan I had, and I was desperate.

"What if we just went for a night?" A night was all I needed. We just needed to be *somewhere else*.

He looked around his bedroom, searching the darkness for what he thought I wanted to hear. I didn't want to be that girl, the one who wasn't forthcoming and caused a huge, stupid misunderstanding. But I couldn't tell Travis the truth about what I'd just proposed to him. He would never agree to go.

"A night?" He clearly had no clue how to respond. He probably thought it was a test, but the only thing I wanted was for him to say yes.

"Marry me," I blurted out.

His mouth parted, forming a silent gasp. I waited

5

lifetimes until his lips curved upward, and he sealed his mouth on mine. His kiss screamed a thousand different emotions. My brain felt swollen with warring thoughts of relief and panic. This was going to work. We would get married, Travis would have an alibi, and everything would be okay.

Oh, hell.

Damn. Shit. *Fuck*.

I was getting married.

Travis

Abby Abernathy was famous for one thing: having no Tell. She could commit a crime and smile like it was any other day, lie without a twitch in her eye. Only one person in the world had any chance of learning her Tell, and that one person had to figure it out if he wanted to have any chance with her.

Me.

Abby had lost her childhood, and I'd lost my mom, so for two people who struggled to get on the same page, we were the same story. That gave me an edge, and after making this my goal over the past months, I'd arrived at an answer:

Abby's Tell was not having one. It might not make sense to most people, but it made perfect sense to me. It was the absence of that Tell that gave her away. The peace in her eyes, the softness in her smile, the relaxation of her shoulders alerted me that something was wrong.

If I didn't know her better, I might have thought this was just our happy ending, but she was up to something. Sitting in the terminal, waiting to board a plane to Vegas, with Abby snuggled into the curve of my body, I knew it was easy to try to ignore. She kept lifting her hand, staring at the ring I'd bought her, and sighing. The middle-aged woman across from us was watching my new fiancée and smiled, probably fantasizing about a time when she had her whole life ahead of her. She didn't know what those sighs really meant, but I had an idea.

It was hard to be happy about what we were about to do with the cloud of so many deaths hanging above our heads. No, really, it was literally above our heads. A television on the wall displayed the local news. Footage of the fire and the latest updates scrolled across the screen. They interviewed Josh Farney. He was covered in soot and he looked horrible, but I was glad to see he'd made it. He was fairly hammered when I saw him before the fight. Most of the people who came to the Circle either came drunk or worked their way up to a buzz while they waited for me and my opponent to trade blows. When the flames began to crawl across the room, adrenaline pumped into everyone's veins—enough to sober up even the most intoxicated.

I wished it hadn't happened. We'd lost so many, and

7

this wasn't exactly something you'd want your wedding to follow. From experience, I knew that the memory of a tragedy could be misplaced. Attaching this date to something we would celebrate year after year would keep it front and center in our minds. Damn, they were still bringing out bodies, and I was acting like this was an annoyance. There were parents out there who had no idea they'd never see their kids again.

That selfish thought led to guilt, and that guilt led to a lie. It was a sheer miracle that we were getting married right now, anyway. But I didn't want Abby thinking I was anything but super fucking pumped about getting married. Knowing her, she'd misread it and then change her mind. So I focused on her, and what we were about to do. I wanted to be a normal, so-excited-I-might-puke groom-to-be, and she deserved nothing less. It wouldn't be the first time I'd pretended not to care about something I couldn't get out of my head. The living proof was snuggled up next to me.

On the television screen, the anchorwoman standing outside Keaton Hall held the microphone with both hands, a frown line between her eyebrows. ". . . what the families of the victims will be asking: who is to blame? Back to you, Kent."

Suddenly the nausea became real. So many had died, of course they were going to hold someone accountable. Was it Adam's fault? Would he go to prison? Would I?

I hugged Abby to me and kissed her hair. A woman behind a desk picked up a mic and began to speak, and my knee started to bounce uncontrollably. If we weren't going to board soon, I might pick up Abby and run to Vegas. I felt like I could have made it there before the plane. The airline agent instructed us about boarding the flight, her voice rising and falling with the scripted announcement she'd probably read a million times. She sounded like the teacher in those *Peanuts* cartoons: bored, monotone, and impossible to understand.

The only thing that made sense were the thoughts on repeat inside my head: I was about to become the husband of the second woman I'd ever loved.

It was almost time. Damn. Shit, yeah! Fuck, yes!

I was getting married!

CHAPTER TWO

The Way Back

Abby

I stared at the sparkling rock on my finger and sighed again. It wasn't the airy sigh a young, newly engaged girl might make while staring at her rather large diamond. It was full of thought. A heavy, thoughtful thought that made me think heavier, thoughtful thoughts. But not second thoughts. We couldn't stay away from each other. What we were about to do was inevitable, and Travis Maddox loved me in a way most people dreamed about. The sigh was filled with worry and hope for my stupid plan. I wanted Travis to be okay so much that it was nearly tangible.

"Stop that, Pidge," Travis said. "You're making me nervous."

"It's just . . . too big."

"It fits just fine," he said, sitting back. We were wedged between a businessman talking softly on his cell phone and an elderly couple. An airline employee was standing behind the gate desk, talking into what looked like a CB radio. I wondered why they didn't just use a regular microphone. She announced a few names, and then hooked the device somewhere on the back of her desk.

"Must be a full flight," Travis said. His left arm was settled on the back of my chair, his thumb gently rubbing my shoulder. He was trying to pretend to be relaxed, but his bobbing knee gave him away.

"The diamond is excessive. I feel like I'm going to get mugged at any moment," I said.

Travis laughed. "First of all, no one is going to fucking touch you. Second, that ring was made to be on your finger. I knew when I saw it—"

"Attention passengers of American flight 2477 to Las Vegas, we are looking for three volunteers to take a later flight. We're offering travel vouchers good for one year from your departure."

Travis looked at me.

"No."

"You in a hurry?" he asked, a smug smile on his face.

I leaned in and kissed him. "Actually, I am." I reached up with my finger and wiped away the smudge of soot under his nose that he'd missed in the shower.

"Thanks, baby," he said, squeezing me against his side. He looked around, his chin lifted, his eyes bright. He was in the best mood I'd seen him in since the night he'd won our bet. It made me smile. Sensible or not, it felt good to be loved so much, and I decided right then and there I would stop apologizing for it. There were worse things than finding your soul mate too early in life, and what was too early, anyway?

"I had a discussion about you with my mom, once," Travis said, looking out the wall of windows to our left. It was still dark. Whatever he saw wasn't on the other side.

"About me? Isn't that kind of . . . impossible?"

"Not really. It was the day she died."

Adrenaline burst from where adrenaline bursts from and sped through my body, pooling in my fingers and toes. Travis had never spoken about his mother to me. I often wanted to ask him about her, but then I thought about the sickening feeling that came over me when someone asked me about my mother, so I never did.

He continued, "She told me to find a girl worth fighting for. The one that doesn't come easy."

I felt a little embarrassed, wondering if that meant I was a huge pain in the ass. Truthfully, I was, but that wasn't the point.

"She said to never stop fighting, and I didn't. She was right." He took a deep breath, seeming to let that thought settle into his bones.

The idea that Travis believed I was the woman who his

mother was talking about, that she would approve of me, made me feel an acceptance I'd never felt before. Diane, who had passed away almost seventeen years before, now made me feel more loved than my own mother.

"I love your mom," I said, leaning against Travis's chest.

He looked down at me, and after a short pause, kissed my hair. I couldn't see his face, but I could hear in his voice how much he was affected. "She would have loved you, too. No doubt in my mind."

The woman spoke into her CB again. "Attention passengers of American flight 2477 to Las Vegas: We will begin boarding soon. We'll start with anyone needing boarding assistance, and those with young children, and then we'll begin boarding first class and business class."

"How about exceptionally tired?" Travis said, standing. "I need a fuckin' Red Bull. Maybe we should have kept our tickets for tomorrow like we'd planned?"

I raised an eyebrow. "You have a problem with me being in a hurry to be Mrs. Travis Maddox?"

He shook his head, helping me to my feet. "Hell no. I'm still in shock, if you wanna know the truth. I just don't want you to be rushing because you're afraid you'll change your mind."

"Maybe I'm afraid you'll change your mind."

Travis's eyebrows pulled in, and he wrapped his arms around me. "You can't really think that. You gotta know there's nothing I want more."

I rose up on the balls of my feet and pecked his lips. "I think we're getting ready to board a plane for Vegas so we can get married, that's what I think."

Travis squeezed me against him, and then kissed me excitedly from cheek to collarbone. I giggled as he tickled my neck, and laughed even louder when he lifted me off the ground. He kissed me one last time before taking my bag off the floor, lowered me to the ground, and then led me by the hand to the line.

We showed our boarding passes and walked down the Jetway hand in hand. The flight attendants took one look at us and offered a knowing smile. Travis passed our seats to let me by, placed our carry-on bags in the overhead bin, and collapsed next to me. "We should probably try to sleep on the way, but I'm not sure I can. I'm too fucking amped."

"You just said you needed a Red Bull."

His dimple caved as he smiled. "Stop listening to everything I say. I'm probably not going to make sense for the next six months while I try to process the fact that I've gotten everything I've ever wanted."

I leaned back to meet his eyes. "Trav, if you wonder why I'm in such a hurry to marry you . . . what you just said is one of the many reasons why."

"Yeah?"

"Yeah."

He scooted down in his seat, and then laid his head on

my shoulder, nuzzling my neck a few times before relaxing. I touched my lips to his forehead, and then looked out the window, waiting as the other passengers passed by and silently praying for the pilot to hurry the hell out of there. I'd never been so thankful for my unrivaled poker face. I wanted to stand up and scream for everyone to sit down and for the pilot to get us off the ground, but I forbid myself to even fidget, and willed my muscles to relax.

Travis's fingers found their way to mine, and intertwined with them. His breath heated up the spot it touched on my shoulder, sending warmth throughout my body. Sometimes I just wanted to drown in him. I thought about what might happen if my plan didn't work. Travis being arrested, tried in court, and the worst case scenario: being sent to prison. Knowing it was possible to be separated from him for a very long time, I felt that a promise to be with him forever didn't seem like enough. My eyes filled with tears, and one escaped, falling down my cheek. I wiped it away quickly. Damn fatigue always made me more emotional.

The other passengers were stowing their bags and buckling their seat belts, going through the motions with no idea that our lives were about to change forever.

I turned to look out the window. Anything to get my mind off the urgency to get off the ground. "Hurry," I whispered.

Travis

It was easy to relax when I rested my head in the crook of Abby's neck. Her hair still smelled a little bit like smoke, and her hands were still pink and swollen from trying to force the basement window open. I tried to push that image from my head: the soot smudges on her face, her frightened eyes red and irritated from the smoke, emphasized by the smeared black mascara surrounding them. If I hadn't stayed behind, she might not have made it. Life without Abby didn't sound like much of a life at all. I didn't want to even wonder what losing her would be like. Going from a nightmare situation to one I'd dreamed about was a jarring experience, but lying there against Abby as the plane hummed and the flight attendant deadpanned the announcements over the PA system made for a somewhat easier transition.

I reached for Abby's fingers, lacing mine with hers. Her cheek pressed against the top of my head so subtly that if I'd been paying attention to what string to pull to trigger the automatic inflation of my life vest, I might have missed her tiny display of affection.

In just a few months' time, the petite woman next to me had become my whole world. I fantasized about how beautiful she would be in her wedding dress, returning home to watch Abby make the apartment her own, buying our first car, and doing those everyday, boring things that married people did, like the dishes and grocery shopping—together. I imagined watching her walk across the stage at her graduation. After we both found jobs, we would likely start a family. That was just three or four years away. We both had broken homes, but I knew Abby would be a damn good mother. I thought about how I would react when she broke the news to me of being pregnant, and I already felt a little emotional about it.

It wouldn't all be sunshine and rainbows, but struggling through a rough patch was when we were at our best, and we'd had enough rough patches to know we could get through them.

With thoughts of a future in which Abby was swollen with our first child running through my mind, my body relaxed against the itchy airplane seat, and I fell asleep.

What was I doing here? The smell of smoke burned my nose, and the cries and screaming in the distance made my blood turn to ice, even though sweat was pouring down my face. I was back in the bowels of Keaton Hall.

"Pigeon?" I yelled. I coughed and squinted my eyes, as if that would help me see through the darkness. "Pigeon!"

I'd felt this feeling before. The panic; the pure adrenaline of being truly afraid of dying. Death was just moments away, but I didn't think about what it would feel like to suffocate or burn alive. I only thought about Abby. Where was she? Was she okay? How would I save her?

A single door came into view, highlighted by the approaching flames. I turned the knob and pushed into the ten-by-ten room. It was just four walls of concrete blocks. One window. A small group of girls and a couple of guys were against the far wall, trying to reach for their only escape.

Derek, one of my frat brothers, was holding up one of the girls, and she was desperately reaching for the window. "Can you get it, Lindsey?" He grunted, breathing hard.

"No! I can't reach it!" she cried, clawing above her. She was wearing a pink Sigma Kappa T-shirt, damp from sweat.

Derek nodded to his friend. I didn't know his name, but he was in my humanities class. "Lift Emily, Todd! She's taller!"

Todd bent over and laced his fingers together, but Emily had flattened herself against the wall, frozen with fear. "Emily, get over here."

Her face compressed. She looked like a little girl. "I want my mom," she whimpered.

"Get. The fuck. Over here!" Todd commanded.

After taking a tiny moment to find her courage, Emily pushed away from the wall and climbed onto Todd. He pushed her up, but she couldn't reach it, either.

Lainey watched her friend reach for the window, noticed the approaching flames, and then balled her hands into fists at her chest. She squeezed them so tight, they shook. "Keep trying, Emily!"

"Let's try another way!" I said, but they didn't hear me. Maybe they'd already tried several routes, and this was the only window they could find. I ran into the dark hallway and looked around. This was the dead end. We had nowhere else to run.

I went back in, trying to think of something to save us. Dusty sheets covered stored furniture that lined the walls, and the fire was using them as a pathway. A pathway straight to the room we were in.

I backed up a few steps, and then turned to face the kids behind me. Their eyes widened, and they retreated against the wall. Lainey was trying to climb up the cement blocks out of pure terror.

"Have you seen Abby Abernathy?" I said. They didn't hear me. "Hey!" I yelled again. None of those kids acknowledged me. I walked up to Derek and screamed at him. "Hey!" He looked right through me at the fire, a horrified look on his face. I looked at the others. They didn't see me, either.

Confused, I walked over to the wall, and jumped, trying to reach the window, and then I was kneeling on the ground outside, looking in. Derek, Todd, Lainey, Lindsey, and Emily were still inside. I tried to open the window, but it wouldn't budge. I kept trying, anyway, hoping at any moment it would pop open and I could pull them out.

"Hold on!" I yelled. "Help!" I yelled again, hoping someone would hear.

The girls hugged, and Emily began to wail. "This is just a bad dream. This is just a bad dream. Wake up! Wake up!" she said over and over.

"Get one of the sheets, Lainey!" Derek said. "Roll it up and shove it under the door!"

Lainey scrambled to pull a sheet off a desk. Lindsey helped her, and then watched Lainey shove it desperately under the door. They both backed away, watching the door.

"We're trapped," Todd said to Derek.

Derek's shoulders fell. Lainey walked over to him, and he touched her dirty cheeks with both hands. They stared into each other's eyes. Thick, black smoke snaked under the door and seeped into the room.

Emily jumped for the window. "Lift me up, Todd! I want out! I want out of here!"

Todd watched her jump with a defeated expression on his face.

"Mommy!" Emily screamed. "Mommy help me!" Her eyes were trained on the window, but still she looked past me.

Lindsey reached out for Emily, but she wouldn't be touched. "Sssh . . ." she said, trying to comfort her from where she stood. She covered her mouth with her hands and began to cough. She looked at Todd, tears streaming down her face. "We're going to die."

"I don't want to die!" Emily screamed, still jumping.

As the smoke filled the room I punched the window, over and over. The adrenaline must have been unbelievable, because I couldn't feel my hand hitting the glass, even though

21

I was using every bit of strength I had. "Help me! Help!" I yelled, but no one came.

Smoke bumped and swirled against the window, and the coughs and crying silenced.

My eyes popped open, and I looked around. I was on the plane with Abby, my hands clenching the armrests, and every muscle in my body clenched.

"Travis? You're sweating," Abby said. She touched my cheek.

"I'll be right back," I said, quickly unbuckling my seat belt. I rushed to the back of the plane and jerked open the lavatory door, and then locked it behind me. Flipping up the sink lever, I splashed water on my face, and then stared into the mirror, watching the drops of water slide off my face and onto the counter.

They were there because of me. I knew Keaton wasn't safe, and I knew too many people were in that basement, and I let it happen. I contributed to dozens of deaths, and now I was on a plane to Las Vegas. What the fuck was wrong with me?

I walked back to my seat and buckled in next to Abby.

She stared at me, noticing right away that something was wrong. "What?"

"It's my fault."

She shook her head, and kept her voice low. "No. Don't do that."

"I should have said no. I should have insisted on a safer place."

"You didn't know that was going to happen." She glanced around, making sure no one was listening. "It's awful. It's horrific. But we couldn't stop it. We can't change it."

"What if I get arrested, Abby? What if I go to jail?"

"Sssh," she said, reminding me of the way Lindsey tried to comfort Emily in my dream. "It won't happen," she whispered. Her eyes were focused; resolute.

"Maybe it should."

CHAPTER THREE

Lucky One

Abby

When the wheels of the airplane touched down on the runway of McCarran International Airport, Travis was finally relaxed and leaning on my shoulder. The bright lights of Las Vegas had been visible for the past ten minutes, signaling us like a beacon toward everything I hated—and everything I wanted.

Travis roused slowly, glancing out the window quickly before kissing the cusp of my shoulder. "We're here?"

"Viva. I thought maybe you'd go back to sleep. It's going to be a long day."

"There's no way I was going back to sleep after that dream," he said, stretching. "I'm not sure I want to sleep again."

My fingers squeezed his. I hated to see him so shaken. He wouldn't talk about his dream, but it didn't take much to figure out where he was while he was sleeping. I wondered if anyone that had escaped from Keaton would be able to close their eyes without seeing the smoke and the panicked faces. The plane arrived at the gate, the SEAT BELT light dinged, and the cabin lights came on, signaling everyone to stand up and dig for their carry-on luggage. Everyone was in a hurry, even though no one was getting out of there before the people seated ahead of them.

I sat, feigning patience, watching Travis stand to pull out our luggage. His T-shirt rose when he reached up, revealing his abs shifting and then contracting when he pulled down the bags.

"You got a dress in here?"

I shook my head. "I thought I'd find one here."

He nodded once. "Yeah, I bet they have plenty to choose from. A better selection for a Vegas wedding than home."

"My line of thinking exactly."

Travis held out his hand and helped me take the two steps to the aisle. "You'll look great no matter what you put on."

I kissed his cheek and took my bag just as the line began to move. We followed the other passengers down the gateway and into the terminal.

"Déjà vu," Travis whispered.

I felt the same. The slot machines sung their siren's song and flashed brightly colored lights, falsely promising luck and big money. The last time Travis and I were here, it was easy to pick out the couples who were getting married, and I wondered if we were just as obvious.

Travis took my hand as we passed baggage claim, and then followed the sign marked TAXIS. The automatic doors parted and we walked into the desert night air. It was still stifling hot, and dry. I breathed in the heat, letting Las Vegas saturate every part of me.

Marrying Travis would be the hardest easiest thing I'd ever done. I needed to awaken the parts of me that were molded in the darkest corners of this city to make my plan work. If Travis thought that I was doing this for any reason other than just wanting to commit to him, he would never let me go through with it, and Travis was not exactly gullible, and worse, he knew me better than anyone else; he knew what I was capable of. If I pulled the wedding off, *and* kept Travis out of prison without him knowing why, it would be my best bluff yet.

Even though we'd bypassed the crowd waiting for baggage, there was a long line for taxis. I sighed. We should have been getting married by now. It was still dark, but it had been over five hours since the fire. We couldn't afford more lines.

"Pidge?" Travis squeezed my hand. "You okay?"

"Yeah," I said, shaking my head and smiling. "Why?"

"You seem . . . a little tense."

I took stock of my body; how I was standing, my facial

expression, anything that might tip him off. My shoulders were so tight they were hanging up around my ears, so I forced them to relax. "I'm just ready."

"To get it over with?" he asked, his eyebrows pulling in infinitesimally. Had I not known better, I would have never caught it.

"Trav," I said, wrapping my arms around his waist. "This was my idea, remember?"

"So was the last time we went to Vegas. You remember how that turned out?"

I laughed, and then I felt terrible. The vertical line his eyebrow formed when he pushed them together deepened. This was so important to him. How much he loved me was overwhelming most of the time, but tonight was different. "I'm in a hurry, yes. Aren't you?"

"Yes, but something's off."

"You're just nervous. Stop worrying."

His face smoothed, and he hugged me. "Okay. If you say you're okay, then I believe you."

Fifteen long minutes later, and we were at the front of the line. A taxi pulled to the curb and stopped. Travis opened the door for me, and I ducked into the backseat and slid over, waiting for him to get in.

The cabdriver looked over his shoulder. "Short trip?"

Travis situated our single carry-on bag in front of him on the floorboard. "We travel light."

"Bellagio, please," I said calmly, keeping the urgency out of my voice.

With lyrics I didn't understand, a cheery, circuslike melody hummed through the speakers as we drove from the airport to the strip. The lights were visible miles before we reached the hotel.

When we arrived at the Strip, I noticed a river of people trekking up and down the sides of the road. Even in the wee hours of the morning, the sidewalks were packed with bachelors, women pushing strollers with sleeping babies, people in costumes taking pictures for tips, and businessmen—apparently looking to unwind.

Travis put his arm around my shoulders. I leaned against him, trying not to look at my watch for the tenth time.

The taxi pulled into the circle drive of the Bellagio, and Travis leaned forward with bills to pay the driver. He then pulled out our roller carry-on, and waited for me. I scooted out, taking his hand and stepping out onto the concrete. As if it weren't in the early AM, people were standing in the taxi line to go to a different casino, and others were returning, weaving and laughing after a long night of drinking.

Travis squeezed my hand. "We're really here."

"Yep!" I said, pulling him inside. The ceiling was distractingly ornate. Everybody in the lobby was standing around with their noses in the air.

"What are you—?" I said, turning to Travis. He was letting me pull him while he took in the ceiling.

"Look, Pidge! It's . . . wow," he said, in awe of the huge, multicolored flowers kissing the ceiling.

"Yep!" I said, tugging him to the front desk.

"Checking in," I said. "And we need to schedule a wedding at a local chapel."

"Which one?" the man asked.

"Any one. A nice one. A twenty-four-hour one."

"We can arrange that. I'll just get you checked in here, and then the concierge can help you with a wedding chapel, shows, anything you'd like."

"Great," I said, turning to Travis with a triumphant grin. He was still staring at the ceiling.

"Travis!" I said, pulling on his arm.

He turned, snapping out of his hypnotic state. "Yeah?"

"Can you go over to the concierge and get the wedding scheduled?"

"Yeah? I mean yeah. I can do that. Which one?"

I laughed once. "Close. Open all night. Classy."

"Got it," he said. He pecked my cheek before pulling the carry-on to the concierge desk.

"We're under Maddox," I said, pulling out a piece of paper. "This is our confirmation number."

"Ah, yes. I have a honeymoon suite available if you'd like to upgrade?"

I shook my head. "We're good." Travis was across the

room, talking with a man behind the desk. They were looking at a brochure together, and he had a huge smile on his face while the man pointed out the different venues.

"Please let this work," I said under my breath.

"What was that, ma'am?"

"Oh. Nothing," I said as he returned to clicking away on his computer.

Travis

Abby leaned in with a smile when I kissed her cheek, and then continued with check-in while I popped over to the concierge to nail down a chapel. I glanced over at my soon-to-be wife, her long legs propped up by those wedge heel shoes that make a nice pair of legs look even nicer. Her flow-y, thin shirt was just see-through enough that I felt disappointed to see a tank top under it. Her favorite sunglasses were perched on the front of her favorite fedora, and just a few long locks of her caramel hair, a little wavy from drying naturally after her shower, were cascading out from under the hat. My God, that woman was fucking sexy. She didn't even have to try, and all I wanted was to be all up in her business. Now that we were engaged that didn't sound like such a bastard thing to think.

"Sir?" the concierge said.

"Oh, yeah. Hey," I said, taking a last glance at Abby

before giving the guy my full attention. "I need a chapel. Open all night. Classy."

He smiled. "Of course, sir. We have several for you right here at the Bellagio. They are absolutely beautiful and—"

"You don't happen to have Elvis at a chapel here, do you? I figure if we're going to get married in Vegas, we should either get married by Elvis, or at least invite him, ya know?"

"No, sir, I apologize, the Bellagio chapels do not offer an Elvis impersonator. However, I can find a few numbers for you to call and request that one appear at your wedding. There is also, of course, the world famous Graceland Chapel, if you prefer. They have packages that include an Elvis impersonator."

"Classy?"

"I'm sure you'll be very pleased."

"Okay, that one. As quickly as possible."

The concierge smiled. "In a hurry, are we?"

I started to grin, but I realized I was already smiling, and probably had been, like an idiot, since I arrived at his desk. "Do you see that girl over there?"

He glanced at her. Quickly. Respectfully. I liked him. "Yes, sir. You're a lucky man."

"I sure as shit am. Schedule the wedding for two . . . maybe three hours from now? She'll need time to pick up a few things and get ready."

32

"Very thoughtful of you, sir." He clicked a few buttons on his keyboard and then grabbed the mouse, moving it around and clicking it a few times. His smile faded as he concentrated, and then it lit up his face again when he finished. The printer buzzed, and then he handed me a piece of paper. "There you are, sir. Congratulations." He held up his fist, and I bumped it, feeling like he'd just handed me a winning lottery ticket.

CHAPTER FOUR

Three Hours

Travis

Abby held my hand, pulling me along as we walked through the casino to the elevators. I was dragging my feet, trying to take a look around before we went upstairs. It had only been a few months since the last time we'd been in Vegas, but this time was less stressful. We were here for a much better reason. Regardless, Abby was still all-business, refusing to pause long enough for me to get too comfortable around the tables. She hated Las Vegas and with good reason, which made me question even more why she chose to come here, but as long as she was on a mission to be my wife, I wasn't going to argue.

"Trav," she said, huffing. "The elevators are right . . . there . . ." She tugged on me a few times toward her final destination.

"We're on vacation, Pidge. Cool your jets."

"No, we're getting married, and we have less than twenty-four hours to get it done."

I pressed the button, pulling us both into an open space to the side of the crowd. It shouldn't have been surprising that there were so many people just ending their night this close to sunrise, but even a buck wild frat boy like myself could be impressed here.

"I still can't believe it," I said. I brought her fingers to my mouth and kissed them.

Abby was still looking above the elevator doors, watching the numbers descend. "You've mentioned that." She looked over to me and one corner of her mouth turned up. "Believe it, baby. We're here."

My chest rose while my lungs filled with air, preparing to let out a long sigh. In recent memory, or maybe ever, my bones and muscles had never been so relaxed. My mind was at ease. It felt strange to feel all of those things, knowing what we'd just left behind back on campus, and at the same time feeling so responsible. It was disorienting, and unsettling, this feeling happy one minute, and like a criminal the next.

A slit formed between the elevator doors, and then they slowly slid away from each other, allowing the passengers to bleed out into the hallway. Abby and I stepped on together with our small roller duffle bag. One woman had a large purse, a large carry-on that was the size of two of ours, and a four-wheeled, vertical suitcase that could fit at least two small children.

"Moving here?" I asked. "That's cool." Abby jammed her elbow into my ribs.

She took a long look at me, and then Abby, and then spoke in a French accent. "No." She looked away, clearly unhappy I'd spoken to her.

Abby and I traded glances, and then she widened her eyes, silently saying *Wow, what a bitch*. I tried not to laugh. Damn, I loved that woman, and I loved that I knew what she was thinking without her saying a word.

The French woman nodded. "Press floor thirty-five, please." Almost the Penthouse. Of course.

When the doors opened on the twenty-fourth floor, Abby and I stepped out onto the ornate carpet, a bit lost, doing the search-walk that people always do when looking for their hotel room. Finally, at the end of the hall, Abby inserted her keycard and pulled it out quickly.

The door clicked. The light turned green. We were in.

Abby flipped on the light and pulled her purse over her head, tossing it on to the king-size bed. She smiled at me. "This is nice."

I let go of the bag handle, letting it topple over, and then took Abby into my arms. "That's it. We're here. When we sleep in that bed later, we're going to be husband and wife."

Abby looked into my eyes, deep and thoughtful, and then cupped one side of my face. A corner of her mouth turned up. "We sure will."

I couldn't begin to imagine what thoughts were swirling behind her beautiful gray eyes, because almost immediately that thoughtful look disappeared.

She rose up on the balls of her feet and pecked me on the mouth. "What time is the wedding?"

Abby

"*Three* hours?" I kept my muscles relaxed even though my entire body wanted to tense up. We were wasting too much time, and I had no way to explain to Travis why I needed to get it over with.

Get it over with? Is that how I really felt about it? Maybe it wasn't just that Travis needed a plausible alibi. Maybe I was afraid I would chicken out if there was too much time to think about what we were doing.

"Yeah," Travis said. "I figured you'd need time to get a dress and your hair done and all that girly shit. Was that . . . was I wrong?"

"No. No, it's fine. I guess I was just thinking we'd get here and just go. But, you're right."

"We're not going to the Red, Pidge. We're gettin' married. I know it's not in a church, but I figured we'd . . . ."

"Yeah." I shook my head and closed my eyes for a second, and then looked at him. "Yes, you're right. I'm sorry. I'll go downstairs, find something white, and then I'll come back here and get ready. If I can't find something here, I'll go to Crystals. There are more shops there."

Travis walked toward me, stopping just a few inches away. He watched me for several moments, long enough to make me squirm.

"Tell me," he said softly. No matter how I tried to explain it away, he knew me well enough to know—poker face or not—that I was hiding something from him.

"I think what you're reading is exhaustion. I haven't slept in almost twenty-four hours."

He sighed, kissed my forehead, and then went to the mini fridge. He bent over, and then turned, holding up two small cans of Red Bull. "Problem solved."

"My fiancé is a genius."

He handed me a can, and then took me into his arms. "I like that."

"That I think you're a genius?"

"Being your fiancé."

"Yeah? Don't get used to it. I'll be calling you something different in three hours."

"I'll like the new name even better."

I smiled, watching Travis open the bathroom door.

"While you find a dress, I'm going to take another shower, shave, and then try to find something to wear."

"So you won't be here when I get back?"

"Do you want me to be? It's at the Graceland Chapel, right? I thought we'd just meet there."

"It'll be kind of cool to see each other at the chapel, just before, dressed and ready to walk down the aisle."

"You're going to walk around Vegas by yourself for three hours?"

"I grew up here, remember?"

Travis thought for a moment. "Isn't Jesse still working as a pit boss?"

I lifted an eyebrow. "I don't know. I haven't talked to him. But even if he was, the only casino I'll be anywhere near is the Bellagio's, and that's just long enough for me to walk through to our room."

Travis seemed satisfied with that, and then nodded. "Meet you there." He winked at me, and then shut the bathroom door.

I grabbed my purse off the bed and the room keycard, and, after glancing at the bathroom door, picked up Travis's cell phone off the nightstand.

Opening his contacts, I pressed on the name I needed, sent the contact information to my phone via text, and then deleted the text message the second it went through. When I set his phone down, the bathroom door opened, and Travis appeared in just a towel.

"Marriage license?" he asked.

"The chapel will take care of it for an extra fee."

Travis nodded, seeming relieved, and then shut the door again.

I yanked the room door open and made my way to the elevator, inputting and then calling the new number.

"Please pick up," I whispered. The elevator opened,

revealing a crowd of young women, probably just a little older than me. They were giggling and slurring their words, half of them discussing their night, the others deciding if they should go to bed or just stay up so they wouldn't miss their flight home.

"Pick up, damnit," I said after the first ring. Three rings later, voicemail chimed in.

You've reached Trent. You know what to do.

"Ugh," I huffed, letting my hand fall to my thigh. The door opened, and I walked with purpose to the Bellagio shops.

After searching through too fancy, too trashy, too much lace, too many beads, and too . . . much of everything, I finally found it: the dress I would wear when I became Mrs. Maddox. It was white, of course, and tea length. Fairly plain, really, except for the sheer bateau neckline and a white satin ribbon that tied around the waist. I stood in the mirror, letting my eyes study each line and detail. It was beautiful, and I felt beautiful in it. In just a couple of hours, I would be standing next to Travis Maddox, watching his eyes take in every curve of the fabric.

I walked along the wall, scanning the numerous veils. After trying on the fourth, I placed it back into its cubby, flustered. A veil was too proper. Too innocent. Another display caught my eye, and I walked toward it, letting my fingers run over the different beads, pearls, stones, and metals of various hairpins. They were less delicate, and

41

more . . . *me*. There were so many on the table, but I kept coming back to one in particular. It had a small, silver comb, and the rest of it was just dozens of different-size rhinestones that somehow formed a butterfly. Without knowing why, I held it in my hand, sure it was perfect.

The shoes were in the back of the store. They didn't have a huge selection, but luckily I wasn't super picky and chose the first pair of silver strappy heels I saw. Two straps went over my toes, and two more around my ankle, with a group of pearls to camouflage the belt. Thankfully they had size six in stock, and I was on to the last thing on my list: jewelry.

I chose a simple but elegant pair of pearl earrings. At the top, where they fastened to my ear, was a small cubic zirconia, just flashy enough for a special occasion, and a matching necklace. Never in my life had I wanted to stand out. Apparently even my wedding wouldn't change that for me.

I thought about the first time I stood in front of Travis. He was sweaty, shirtless, and panting, and I was covered in Marek Young's blood. That was just six months ago, and now we're getting married. And I'm nineteen. I'm only nineteen.

What the fuck am I doing?

I stood at the register, watching the receipt being printed out for the dress, shoes, hairpin, and jewelry, trying not to hyperventilate.

The redhead behind the counter tore off the receipt and handed it to me with a smile. "It's a gorgeous dress. Nice choice."

"Thank you," I said. I wasn't sure if I smiled back or not. Suddenly dazed, I walked away, holding the bag against my chest.

After a quick stop into the jewelry store for a black titanium wedding ring for Travis, I glanced at my phone and then tossed it back into my purse. I was making good time.

When I walked into the casino, my purse began to vibrate. I placed the bag between my legs and reached for it. After two rings, my searching fingers grew desperate, clawing and shoving everything to the side to get to the phone in time.

"Hello?" I screeched. "Trent?"

"Abby? Is everything okay?"

"Yeah," I breathed as I sat on the floor against the side of the closest slot machine. "We're fine. How are you?"

"I've been sitting with Cami. She's pretty upset about the fire. She lost some of her regulars."

"Oh, God, Trent. I'm so sorry. I can't believe it. It doesn't seem real," I said, my throat feeling tight. "There were so many. Their parents probably don't even know, yet." I held my hand to my face.

"Yeah." He sighed, sounding tired. "It's like a war zone down there. What's that noise? Are you in an arcade?" He sounded disgusted, as if he already knew the answer, and he couldn't believe we were that insensitive. "What?" I said. "God, no. We . . . we hopped on a flight to Vegas."

"*What?*" he said, incensed. Or maybe just confused, I couldn't be sure. He was excitable.

I cringed at the disapproval in his voice, knowing it was just the beginning. I had an objective. I had to set my feelings aside as best I could until I achieved what I came for. "Just listen. It's important. I don't have a lot of time, and I need your help."

"Okay. With what?"

"Don't talk. Just listen. Promise?"

"Abby, stop playin'. Just fucking tell me."

"There were a lot of people at the fight last night. A lot of people died. Someone has got to go to prison for it."

"You thinkin' it's gonna be Travis?"

"Him and Adam, yeah. Maybe John Savage, and anyone else they think coordinated it. Thank God Shepley wasn't in town."

"What do we do?"

"I asked Travis to marry me."

"Uh . . . okay. How the hell is that going to help him?"

"We're in Vegas. Maybe if we can prove we were off getting married a few hours later, even if a few dozen drunken frat boys testify that he was at the fight, it will sound just crazy enough to create reasonable doubt."

"Abby." He sighed.

A sob caught in my throat. "Don't say it. If you don't think it'll work, just don't tell me, okay? It was all I could think of, and if he finds out why I'm doing this, he won't do it."

"Of course he won't. Abby, I know you're afraid, but this is crazy. You can't marry him to keep him out of trouble. This won't work, anyway. You didn't leave until after the fight. "

"I said not to say that."

"I'm sorry. He wouldn't want you to do this, either. He would want you to marry him because you want to. If he ever found out, it'd break his heart."

"Don't be sorry, Trent. It's going to work. At least it will give him a chance. It's a chance, right? Better odds than he had."

"I guess," he said, sounding defeated.

I sighed and then nodded, covering my mouth with my free hand. Tears blurred my vision, making a kaleidoscope out of the casino floor. A chance was better than nothing.

"Congratulations," he said.

"Congrats!" Cami said in the background. Her voice sounded tired and hoarse, even though I was sure she was sincere.

"Thank you. Keep me updated. Let me know if they come sniffing around the house, or if you hear anything about an investigation."

"Will do . . . and it's really fucking weird that our baby brother is the first to get married."

I laughed once. "Get over it."

"Fuck off. And, I love ya."

"Love you, too, Trent."

I held the phone in my lap with both hands, watching the people walking by stare at me. They were obviously wondering why I was sitting on the floor, but not enough to ask. I stood up, picked up my purse and bag, and inhaled a deep breath.

"Here comes the bride," I said, taking my first steps.

CHAPTER FIVE

Caught

Travis

I dried off, brushed my teeth, and slipped on a T-shirt and shorts, and then my Nikes. Ready. Damn, it was good to be a man. I couldn't imagine having to blow-dry my hair for half an hour, and then burn it with whatever handheld metal hot iron I could find, and then spend fifteen to twenty minutes getting my makeup just right before finally getting dressed. Key. Wallet. Phone. Out the door. Abby had said there were shops downstairs, but she hinted strongly that we shouldn't see each other until the wedding, so I headed for the Strip.

Even when in a hurry, if the Bellagio fountains are dancing to the music, it is un-American not to stop and stand in awe. I lit a cigarette and puffed on it, resting my arms on a large, concrete ledge that lined the viewing platform. Watching the water sway and spray to the music reminded me of the last time I was there, standing with

Shepley while Abby efficiently kicked the asses of four or five poker veterans.

Shepley. Damn, I was so glad he wasn't at that fight. If I'd have lost him, or if he'd lost America, I'm not sure Abby and I would have been here. A loss like that would change the whole dynamic of our friendships. Shepley couldn't be around Abby and me without America, and America couldn't be around us without Shepley. Abby couldn't not be around America. If they hadn't decided to stay with his parents over spring break, I could be suffering the loss of Shepley instead of preparing for our wedding. Thoughts of calling Uncle Jack and Aunt Deana with news of their only son's death made a cold shiver crawl down my spine.

I shook the thought away as I remembered the moment before I called my dad's phone, standing in front of Keaton, the smoke billowing out of the windows. Some of the fire-fighters were holding the hose to pour water inside, others were bringing out survivors. I remembered what it felt like: knowing that I was going to have to tell my dad that Trent was missing and probably dead. How my brother had run the wrong way in the confusion, and Abby and I were standing outside without him. Thoughts of what that would have done to my dad, to our entire family, made me feel sick to my stomach. Dad was the strongest man I knew, but he couldn't take losing anyone else.

My dad and Jack ran our town when they were in high school. They were the first generation of badass Maddox brothers. In college towns, the locals either started fights or were picked on. Jim and Jack Maddox never experienced the latter, and even met and married the only two girls at their college that could handle them: Deana and Diane Hempfling. Yes, sisters, making Shepley and me double cousins. It was probably just as well that Jack and Deana stopped at one, with Mom having five unruly boys. Statistically, our family was due for a girl, and I'm not sure the world could handle a female Maddox. All the fight and anger, plus estrogen? Everyone would die.

When Shepley was born, Uncle Jack settled down. Shepley was a Maddox, but he had his mother's temperament. Thomas, Tyler, Taylor, Trenton, and I all had short fuses like our dad, but Shepley was calm. We were the best of friends. He was a brother who lived in a different house. He pretty much was, but he looked more like Thomas than the rest of us. We all shared the same DNA.

The fountain died down and I walked away, seeing the sign for Crystals. If I could get in and out of there quick, maybe Abby would still be in the Bellagio shops and wouldn't see me.

I picked up the pace, dodging the extremely drunk and tired tourists. One short escalator ride and a bridge later, I was inside the stories-tall shopping center. It had glass rectangles displaying colorful water tornados, high-end shops, and the same odd range of people. Families to strippers. Only in Vegas.

I popped in and out of one suit shop without any luck, and then walked until I hit a Tom Ford store. In ten minutes, I'd found and tried on the perfect gray suit but had trouble finding a tie. "Fuck it," I said, taking the suit and a white button-up to the register. Who said a groom had to wear a tie?

Walking out of the shopping center, I saw a pair of black Converse in the window. I went in, asked for my size, tried them on, and smiled. "I'll take them," I said to the woman helping me. She smiled with a look in her eyes that would have turned me on just six months ago. A woman looking at me that way usually meant any attempts I made to get in her pants had just been made a thousand times easier. That look meant: take me home.

"Great choice," she said in a smooth, flirtatious voice. Her dark hair was long, thick, and shiny. Probably half of her five feet. She was a sophisticated, Asian beauty, wrapped in a tight dress and sky-high heels. Her eyes were sharp, calculating. She was exactly the kind of challenge my old self would have happily taken on. "Are you staying in Vegas long?"

"Just a few days."

"Is this your first time here?"

"Second."

"Oh. I was going to offer to show you around."

"I'm getting married in these shoes in a couple of hours."

My response snuffed out the desire in her eyes, and she smiled pleasantly, but she'd clearly lost interest. "Congratulations."

"Thanks," I said, taking my receipt and bag with the shoe box inside.

I left, feeling much better about myself than I would have had I been here on a guys' trip and leading her back to my hotel room. I didn't know about love back then. It was fanfuckingtastic to go home to Abby every night, and see the welcoming, loving look in her eyes. Nothing was better than coming up with new ways to make her fall in love with me all over again. I lived for that shit now, and it was way more satisfying.

Within an hour of leaving the Bellagio, I had picked up a suit and a gold band for Abby, and was right back where I started: in our hotel room. I sat on the end of the bed and grabbed the remote, clicking on the power to the TV before bending over to untie my sneakers. A familiar scene lit up the screen. It was Keaton, quartered off with yellow tape, and still smoking. The brick around the windows were charred, and the ground surrounding was saturated with water.

The reporter was interviewing a tearful girl, describing how her roommate had never returned to the dorm, and she was still waiting to hear if she was among the dead. I couldn't hold it in anymore. I covered my face with my hands and rested my elbows on my knees. My body shook as I mourned my friends and all the people I didn't know who'd lost their lives, as I apologized over and over for being the reason why they were there, and being too much of a fucking bastard for choosing Abby over turning myself in. When I couldn't cry anymore, I retreated to the shower, standing under the steaming water until I got back into the frame of mind Abby needed me to be in.

She didn't want to see me until just before the wedding, so I got my shit straight in my head, got dressed, slapped on some cologne, tied my new kicks, and headed out. Before letting the door close, I took one long, last look at the room. The next time I came through this door, I'd be Abby's husband. That was the only thing that made the guilt bearable. My heart began to pound. The rest of my life was just hours away.

The elevator opened, and I followed the loudly patterned carpet through the casino. The suit made me feel like a million bucks, and people were staring, wondering where the fine-looking asshole sporting Converse was off to. When I was about halfway through the casino, I noticed a woman sitting on the floor with shopping bags, crying into her cell phone. I stopped dead in my tracks. It was Abby.

Instinctively, I stepped to the side, partially hiding myself at the end of a row of slot machines. With the music, the beeping, and the chatter, I couldn't hear what she was saying, but my blood ran cold. Why was she crying? Who was she crying to? Didn't she want to marry me? Should I confront her? Should I just wait it out and hope to God she doesn't call it off?

Abby picked herself off the floor, struggling with her bags. Everything in me wanted to run to her and help, but I was afraid. I was fucking terrified that if I approached her in that moment, she might tell me the truth, and I was afraid to hear it. The selfish bastard in me took over, and I let her walk away.

Once she was out of sight, I sat on an empty slot machine stool and pulled the pack of cigarettes out of my inside pocket. Flicking the lighter, the end of my cigarette sizzled before it glowed red while I pulled in a long drag of smoke. What was I going to do if Abby changed her mind? Could we come back from something like that? Regardless of the answer, I was going to have to figure out a way. Even if she couldn't go through with the wedding, I couldn't lose her.

I sat there for a long time, smoking, slipping dollar bills into the slot machine while a waitress brought me free drinks. After four, I waved her away. Getting drunk before the wedding wouldn't solve a damn thing. Maybe that's why Abby was having second thoughts. Loving her wasn't enough. I needed to grow the fuck up, get a real job, quit drinking, fighting, and control my goddamn anger. I sat alone in the casino, silently vowing that I would make all of those changes, and they would start right then.

My phone chimed. Just an hour was left before the wedding. I texted Abby, worried how she might respond.

I miss u

Abby

I smiled at the phone display, seeing the text was from Travis. I clicked a response, knowing that words couldn't convey what I was feeling.

I miss u too

T-minus one hour. U ready yet?

Not yet. U?

Hells yes. I look ducking amazing. When u c me u will want 2 marry me 4 sure.

Ducking?

Fucking* goddamn auto correct. Pic?

No! It's bad luck!

Ur lucky 13. You have good luck.

Ur marrying me. So clearly u don't. And don't call me that.

Love u baby.

Love u too. See u soon.

Nervous?

Of course. Aren't you?

Only about ur cold feet.

Feet r toasty warm.

I wish I could explain to u how happy I am right now.

U don't have to. I can relate.

☺

<3

I sat the phone on the bathroom counter and looked into the mirror, touching the end of the lip gloss wand to my bottom lip. After pinning one last piece of my hair back, I went over to the bed, where I'd laid the dress. It wasn't what my ten-year-old self would have chosen, but it was beautiful, and what we were about to do was beautiful. Even why I was doing it was beautiful. I could think of much less noble reasons to get married. And, besides that, we loved each other. Was getting married this young so awful? People used to do this all the time.

I shook my head, trying to shake off the dozens of conflicting emotions swirling around my mind. Why go back and forth? This was happening, and we were in love. Crazy? Yes. Wrong? No.

I stepped into the dress and then pulled up the zipper, standing in front of the mirror. "Much better," I said. In the store, as lovely as the dress was, without hair and makeup done, the dress didn't look right. With my red lips and painted lashes, the look was complete.

I pinned the diamond butterfly into the base of the messy curls that made up my side bun, and slipped my feet into the new strappy pumps. Purse. Phone. Trav's ring. The chapel would have everything else. The taxi was waiting.

Even though thousands of women were married in Las Vegas every year, it didn't keep everyone from staring at me as I walked across the casino floor in my wedding dress. Some smiled, some just watched, but it all made me uncomfortable. When my father lost his last professional match after four in a row, and he announced publicly that it was my fault, I'd received enough attention to last two lifetimes. Because of a few words spoken in frustration, he'd created "Lucky Thirteen" and given me an unbelievable burden to bear. Even when my mother finally decided to leave Mick and we moved to Wichita three years later, starting over seemed impossible. I enjoyed two whole weeks of being an unknown before the first local reporter figured out who I was and approached me on the front lawn of my high school. All it took was one hateful girl a single hour of Friday Night Googling to figure out why anyone in the press cared enough to try to get a "Where Is She Now?" headline. The second half of my high school experience was ruined. Even with a mouthy, scrappy best friend.

When America and I left for college, I wanted to be invisible. Until the day I'd met Travis, I was enjoying my newfound anonymity immensely.

I looked down from the hundredth pair of eyes watching me intently, and I wondered if being with Travis would always make me feel conspicuous.

CHAPTER SIX

Dead or Alive

Travis

The limo door slammed hard behind me. "Oh, shit. Sorry. I'm nervous."

The driver waved me away. "No problem. Twenty-two dollars, please. I'll come back with the limo."

The limo was new. White. Abby would like it. I handed him thirty. "So you'll be right back here in an hour and a half, right?"

"Yes, sir! Never late!"

He drove away, and I turned around. The chapel was lit up, glowing against the early morning sky. It was maybe a half hour before sunrise. I smiled. Abby was going to love it.

The front door opened, and a couple came out. They were middle-aged, but he was in a tux, and she was in a huge wedding dress. A short woman in a light pink suit dress was waving them good-bye, and then she noticed me.

"Travis?"

"Yes," I said, buttoning my jacket.

"I could just eat you up! I hope your bride appreciates what a looker you are!"

"She's prettier than me."

The woman cackled. "I'm Chantilly. Pretty much run things around here." She put her fists at her side, somewhere in the area of her hips. She was as wide as she was tall, and her eyes were nearly hidden under thick, fake lashes. "Come on in, sugar! Come in! Come in!" she said, rushing me inside.

The receptionist at the desk offered a smile and a small stack of paperwork. Yes, we want a DVD. Yes, we want flowers. Yes, we want Elvis. I checked all of the appropriate boxes, filled in our names and information, and then handed the paper back.

"Thank you, Mr. Maddox," the receptionist said.

My hands were sweating. I couldn't believe I was here.

Chantilly patted my arm, well, more like my wrist, because that's the highest she could reach. "This way, honey. You can freshen up and wait for your bride in here. What was her name?"

"Uh . . . Abby . . ." I said, walking through the door Chantilly had opened. I looked around, noting the couch and mirror surrounded by a thousand huge lightbulbs. The wallpaper was busy but nice, and everything seemed clean and classy, just like Abby wanted.

"I'll let you know when she arrives," Chantilly said with a wink. "You need anything? A water?"

"Yes, that would be great," I said, sitting down.

"Be right back," she lilted as she backed out of the room and closed the door behind her. I could hear her humming down the hall.

I leaned back against the couch, trying to process what had just happened, and wondering if Chantilly had just chugged a 5-hour ENERGY, or if she was just naturally that chipper. Even though I was just sitting, my heart was pounding against my chest. This is why people had witnesses: to help them keep calm before the wedding. For the first time since we'd landed, I wished Shepley and my brothers were there with me. They would have been giving me all kinds of shit, helping to keep my mind off the fact that my stomach was begging to throw up.

The door opened. "Here you are! Anything else? You look a little nervous. Have you eaten?"

"Nope. I haven't had time."

"Oh, we can't have you passing out at the altar! I'll bring you some cheese and crackers, and maybe a little fruit plate?"

"Uh, sure, thanks," I said, still a little bewildered by Chantilly's enthusiasm.

She backed out, shut the door, and I was alone again. My head fell back against the couch, my eyes picked out different shapes in the wall texture. I was grateful for anything that kept me from glancing down at my watch. Was she coming? I closed my eyes tight, refusing to go there.

She loved me. I trusted her. She would be here. Goddammit, I wished my brothers were here. I was going to go out of my everlovin' mind.

Abby

"Oh, don't you look pretty," the driver said as I slid into the backseat of the taxi.

"Thank you," I said, feeling relieved to be out of the casino. "Graceland Chapel, please."

"Did you want to start out the day married, or what?" the driver said, smiling back at me from the rearview mirror. She had short, gray hair, and her backside filled up all of the seat, and then some.

"It was just the quickest we could get it done."

"You're awfully young to be in such a hurry."

"I know," I said, watching Las Vegas pass by outside my window.

She clicked her tongue. "You look pretty nervous. If you're having second thoughts, just let me know. I don't mind turning around. It's okay, honey."

"I'm not nervous about getting married."

"No?"

"No, we love each other. I'm not nervous about that. I just want him to be okay."

"You think he's having second thoughts?"

"No," I said, laughing once. I met her eyes in the mirror. "Are you married?"

"Once or twice," she said, winking at me. "I got married in the same chapel that you are the first time around. But so did Bon Jovi."

"Oh, yeah?"

"You know Bon Jovi? *Tommy used to work on the docks*!" she sang, very much to my surprise.

"Yep! Heard of him," I said, amused and grateful for the distraction.

"I just love him. Here! I have the CD." She popped it in, and for the rest of the drive we listened to Jon's greatest hits. "Wanted Dead or Alive," "Always," "Bed of Roses"; "I'll Be There for You" was just finishing up as we pulled over to the curb in front of the chapel.

I pulled out a fifty. "Keep the rest. Bon Jovi helped."

She gave me back the change. "No tip, honey. You let me sing."

I shut the door and waved to her as she left. Was Travis already here? I walked up to the chapel and opened the door. An older woman with big hair and too much lip gloss greeted me. "Abby?"

"Yes," I said, fidgeting with my dress.

"You're stunning. My name is Chantilly, and I'll be one of your witnesses. Let me take your things. I'll put them away, and they'll be safe until you're finished."

"Thank you," I said, watching her take away my purse. Something swished when she walked, though I couldn't pinpoint what exactly. "Oh, wait! The . . ." I said, watching as she walked toward me holding out my purse. "Travis's ring is in there. I'm sorry."

Her eyes were barely slits when she smiled, making her fake lashes even more noticeable. "It's fine, honey. Just breathe."

"I don't remember how," I said, sliding his ring over my thumb.

"Here," she said, holding out her hand. "Give me your ring and his. I'll give them to each of you when it's time. Elvis will be by shortly to take you down the aisle."

I looked at her, blank faced. "Elvis."

"As in The King?"

"Yes, I know who Elvis is, but . . ." My words trailed away as I pulled off my ring with a small tug, and placed it in her palm next to Travis's ring.

Chantilly smiled. "You can use this room to freshen up. Travis is waiting, so Elvis will be knocking any minute. See you at the end of the aisle!"

She watched me as she shut the door. I turned, startled by my own reflection in the huge mirror behind me. It was bordered by large, round lights like one an actress might use before a Broadway show. I sat down at the vanity, staring at myself in the mirror. Is that what I was? An actress?

He was waiting. Travis is at the end of the aisle, waiting for me to join him so we can promise the rest of our lives to each other.

What if my plan doesn't work? What if he goes to prison and this was all for nothing? What if they didn't so much as sniff in Travis's direction, and this was all pointless? I no longer had the excuse that I had gotten married, before I was even legal to drink, because I was saving him. Did I need an excuse if I loved him? Why did anyone get married? For love? We had that in spades. I was so sure of everything in the beginning. I used to be sure about a lot things. I didn't feel sure now. About anything.

I thought about the look on Travis's face if he found out the truth, and then I thought about what bailing would do to him. I never wanted him to hurt and I needed him as if he were a part of me. Of those two things I was sure.

Two knocks on the door nearly sent me into a panic attack. I turned, gripping the top of the chair back. It was white wire, swirls and curves formed a heart in the middle.

"Miss?" Elvis said in a deep, southern voice. "It's time."

"Oh," I said quietly. I don't know why. He couldn't hear me.

"Abby? Your hunka hunka burnin' love is ready for ya."

I rolled my eyes. "I just . . . need a minute."

The other side of the door was quiet. "Everything okay?"

"Yes," I said. "Just one minute, please."

After a few more minutes, there was another knock on the door. "Abby?" It was Chantilly. "Can I come in, honey?"

"No. I'm sorry, but no. I'll be okay. I just need a little more time, and I'll be ready."

After another five minutes, three knocks on the door caused beads of sweat to form along my hairline. These knocks were familiar. Stronger. More confident.

"Pidge?"

CHAPTER SEVEN

Cash

Travis

The door blew open. "She's here! I just showed her to a dressing room to freshen up. Are you ready?"

"Yeah!" I said, jumping to my feet. I wiped my sweaty palms on my slacks and followed Chantilly out to the hallway, and into the lobby. I stopped.

"This way, honey," Chantilly said, encouraging me toward the double doors that led into the chapel.

"Where is she?" I asked.

Chantilly pointed. "In there. As soon as she's ready, we'll get started. But, you have to be at the other end of the aisle, sugar."

Her smile was sweet and patient. I imagined she dealt with all kinds of situations, from drunks to jitters. After one last look at the door to Abby's room, I followed Chantilly down the aisle and she gave me the rundown on where to stand. While she was talking, a man with thick chops and an Elvis costume pushed open the door in grandiose fashion, curling his lips and humming "Blue Hawaii."

"Man, I really like Vegas! You like Vegas?" he said, his Elvis impression spot-on.

I grinned. "Today I do."

"Can't ask for better than that! Has Ms. Chantilly told you everything you need to know to be a mister this mornin'?"

"Yeah. I think."

He slapped my back. "No worries, fella, you're gonna do just fine. I'll go get your missus. Be back in a flash."

Chantilly giggled. "Oh, that Elvis." After a couple of minutes, Chantilly checked her watch, and then walked back down the aisle toward the double doors.

"This happens all the time," the officiant assured me.

After another five minutes, Chantilly popped her head through the doors. "Travis? I think she's a little . . . nervous. Do you want to try to talk to her?"

Fuck. "Yeah," I said. The aisle seemed short before, but now it felt like a mile. I pushed through the doors, and raised my fist. I paused, took a breath, and then knocked a few times. "Pidge?"

After what felt like two eternities, Abby finally spoke, her voice on the other side of the door. "I'm here." Even though she was only inches away, she sounded miles away, just like the morning after I brought those two girls home from the bar. Just the thought of that night made me feel a burning sickness in my gut. I didn't even feel like the same person I was then.

"You okay, baby?" I asked.

"Yes. I just . . . I was rushed. I need a moment to breathe."

She sounded anything but okay. I was determined to keep my head, to fight away the panic that used to cause me to do all kinds of stupid stuff. I needed to be the man Abby deserved. "You sure that's all?"

She didn't reply.

Chantilly cleared her throat and wrung her hands, clearly trying to think of something encouraging to say.

I needed to be on the other side of that door.

"Pidge . . ." I said, followed by a pause. What I would say next could change everything, but making everything all right for Abby trumped my own epically selfish needs. "I know you know I love you. What you may not know is that there is nothing I want more than to be your husband. But if you're not ready, I'll wait for you, Pigeon. I'm not going anywhere. I mean, yeah. I want this, but only if you do. I just . . . I need you to know that you can open this door and we can walk down the aisle, or we can get a taxi and go home. Either way, I love you."

After another long pause, I knew it was time. I pulled an old, worn envelope from my inside jacket pocket, and held it with both hands. The faded pen looped around, and I followed the lines with my index finger. My mother had written the words *To the future Mrs. Travis Maddox*. My dad had given it to me when he thought things between Abby and me were getting serious. I'd only pulled this letter out once since then, wondering what she'd written inside, but never betraying the seal. Those words weren't meant for me.

My hands were shaking. I had no clue what Mom had written, but I really needed her right now, and was hoping that this one time, she could somehow reach out from where she was and help me. I squatted down, sliding the envelope under the door.

Abby

Pidge. The word used to make my eyes roll. I didn't know why he started calling me that in the first place, and I didn't care. Now, Travis's weird little nickname for me spoken in his deep, gritty voice made my entire body relax. I stood and walked over to the door, holding my palm to the wood. "I'm here."

I could hear my breath; wheezing, slow, like I was sleeping. Every part of me was relaxed. His warm words fell slowly around me like a cozy blanket. It didn't matter what happened after we got home, as long as I was Travis's wife. It was then that I understood that whether I was doing this to help him or not, I was there to get married to the man who loved me more than any man loved any woman. And I loved him—enough for three lifetimes. In the Graceland Chapel, in this dress was almost exactly where I wanted to be. The only place better would be next to him at the end of the aisle.

Just then, a small, white square appeared at my feet.

"What's this?" I said, bending down to pick it up. The paper was old, yellow. It was addressed to the future Mrs. Travis Maddox.

"It's from my mom," Travis said.

My breath caught. I almost didn't want to open it, it had obviously been sealed and kept safe for so long.

"Open it," Travis said, seeming to read my thoughts.

My finger carefully slid in between the opening, hoping to preserve it as best I could, but failing miserably. I pulled out the tri-folded paper, and the entire world stopped.

We don't know each other, but I know that you must be very special. I can't be there today, to watch my baby boy promise his love to you, but there are a few things that I think I might say to you if I were.

First, thank you for loving my son. Of all my boys, Travis is the most tender hearted. He is also the strongest. He will love you with everything he has for as long as you let him. Tragedies in life sometimes change us, but some things never change.

A boy without a mother is a very curious creature. If Travis is anything like his father, and I know that he is, he's a deep ocean of fragility, protected by a thick wall of swear words and feigned indifference. A Maddox boy will take you all the way to the edge, but if you go with him, he'll follow you anywhere.

I wish more than anything that I could be there today. I wish I could see his face when he takes this step with you, and that I could stand there with my husband and experience this day with all of you. I think that's one of the things I'll miss the most. But today isn't about me. You reading this letter means that my son loves you. And when a Maddox boy falls in love, he loves forever.

Please give my baby boy a kiss for me. My wish for both of you is that the biggest fight you have is over who is the most forgiving.

Love,
Diane

"Pigeon?"

I held the letter to my chest with one hand, and opened the door with the other. Travis's face was tight with worry, but the second his eyes met mine, the worry fell away.

He seemed stunned by the sight of me. "You're . . . I don't think there's a word for how beautiful you are."

His sweet, chestnut eyes, shadowed by his thick eyelashes, soothed my nerves. His tattoos were hidden under his gray suit and crisp, white button-up. My God, he was perfection. He was sexy, he was brave, he was tender, and Travis Maddox was mine. All I had to do was walk down the aisle. "I'm ready."

"What did she say?" he asked.

My throat tightened so a sob wouldn't escape. I kissed him on the cheek. "That's from her."

"Yeah?" he said, a sweet smile sweeping his face.

"And she pretty much nailed everything wonderful about you, even though she didn't get to watch you grow up. She's so wonderful, Travis. I wish I could have known her."

"I wish she could have known you." He paused a moment in thought, and then held up his hands.

His sleeve inched back, revealing his PIGEON tattoo. "Let's sleep on it. You don't have to decide right now. We'll go back to the hotel, think about it, and—" He sighed, letting his arms and shoulders fall. "I know. This is crazy. I just wanted it so bad, Abby. This crazy is my sanity. We can . . ."

I couldn't stand watching him stumble and struggle any longer. "Baby, stop," I said, touching his mouth with three of my fingertips. "Just stop."

He watched me. Waiting.

"Just so we're straight, I'm not leaving here until you're my husband."

At first his brows pulled in, dubious, and then he offered a cautious smile. "You're sure?"

"Where's my bouquet?"

"Oh!" Chantilly said, distracted by the discussion. "Here, honey." She handed me a perfectly round ball of red roses.

Elvis offered his arm, and I took it. "See you at the altar, Travis," he said.

Travis took my hand, kissed my fingers, and then jogged back the way he'd come, followed by a giggly Chantilly.

That small touch wasn't enough. Suddenly I couldn't wait to get to him, and my feet quickly made their way to the chapel. The wedding march wasn't playing, instead "Thing for You," the song we danced to at my birthday party, came through the speakers.

I stopped and looked at Travis, finally getting a chance to take in his gray suit and black Converse sneakers. He smiled when he saw the recognition in my eyes. I took another step, and then another. The officiant gestured for me to slow down, but I couldn't. My entire body needed to be next to Travis more than it ever had been before. He must have felt the same way. Elvis hadn't made it halfway before Travis decided to stop waiting and walked toward us. I took his arm.

"Uh . . . I was gonna give 'er away."

Travis's mouth pulled to one side. "She was already mine."

I hugged his arm, and we walked the rest of the way together. The music quieted, and the officiant nodded to both of us.

"Travis . . . Abby."

Chantilly took my rose bouquet, and then stood to the side.

Our trembling hands were knotted together. We were both so nervous and happy that it was almost impossible to stand still.

Even knowing how much I truly wanted to marry Travis, my hands were trembling. I'm not sure what the officiant said exactly. I can't remember his face or what he wore, I can only recall his deep nasally voice, his northeastern accent, and Travis's hands holding mine.

"Look at me, Pidge," Travis said quietly.

I glanced up at my future husband, getting lost in the sincerity and adoration in his eyes. No one, not even America, had ever looked at me with that much love. The corners of Travis's mouth turned up, so I must have had the same expression.

As the officiant spoke, Travis's eyes poured over me, my face, my hair, my dress—he even looked down at my shoes. Then, he leaned over until his lips were just a few inches from my neck, and inhaled.

The officiant paused.

"I wanna remember everything," Travis said.

The officiant smiled, nodded, and continued.

A flash went off, startling us. Travis glanced behind him, acknowledged the photographer, and then looked at me. We mirrored each other's cheesy grins. I didn't care that we must have looked absolutely ridiculous. It was like we were getting ready to jump off the highest high dive into the deepest river that fed into the most magnificent, terrifying waterfall, right onto the best and most fantastic roller coaster in the universe. Times ten.

"True marriage begins well before the wedding day," the officiant began. "And the efforts of marriage continue well beyond the ceremony's end. A brief moment in time and the stroke of the pen are all that is needed to create the legal bond of marriage, but it takes a lifetime of love, commitment, forgiveness, and compromise to make marriage durable and everlasting. I think, Travis and Abby, you've just shown us what your love is capable of in a tense moment. Your yesterdays were the path that led you to this chapel, and your journey to a future of togetherness becomes a little clearer with each new day."

Travis leaned his cheek to my temple. I was grateful he wanted to touch me where and whenever he could. If I could have hugged him to me and not disrupted the ceremony, I would have. The officiant's words began to blur together. A few times, Travis spoke, and I did, too. I slipped Travis's black ring onto his finger, and he beamed.

"With this ring, I thee wed," I said, repeating after the officiant.

"Nice choice," Travis said, admiring his ring.

When it was Travis's turn, he seemed to have trouble, and then slid two rings onto my finger: my engagement ring, and a simple, gold band.

I wanted to take a moment to appreciate that he'd gotten me an official wedding band, maybe even say so, but I was having an out-of-body experience. The harder I tried to be present, the faster everything seemed to happen.

I thought maybe I should actually listen to the list of things I was promising, but the only voice that made sense was Travis's. "I damn sure do," he said with a smile. "And I promise to never enter another fight, drink in excess, gamble, or throw a punch in anger . . . and I'll never, ever make you cry sad tears again."

When it was my turn again, I paused. "I just want you to know, before I make my promises, that I'm super stubborn. You already know I'm hard to live with, and you've made it clear on dozens of occasions that I drive you crazy. And I'm sure I've driven anyone who's watched these last few months crazy with my indecision and uncertainty. But I want you to know that whatever love is, this has got to be it. We were best friends first, and we tried not to fall in love, and we did anyway. If you're not with me, it's not where I want to be. I'm in this. I'm with you. We might be impulsive, and absolutely insane to be standing here at our age, six months after we met.

This whole thing might play out to be a completely wonderful, beautiful disaster, but I want that if it's with you."

"Like Johnny and June," Travis said, his eyes a bit glossed over. "It's all uphill from here, and I'm going to love every minute of it."

"Do you—" the officiant began.

"I do," I said.

"Okay," he said with a chuckle, "but I have to say it."

"I've heard it once. I don't need to hear it again," I said, smiling, never taking my eyes from Travis. He squeezed my hands. We repeated more promises, and then the officiant paused.

"That's it?" Travis asked.

The officiant smiled. "That's it. You're married."

"Really?" he asked, his eyebrows raised. He looked like a kid on Christmas morning.

"You may now kiss your—"

Travis took me in both arms and wrapped me tightly, kissing me, excitedly and passionate at first, and then his lips slowed, moving against mine more tenderly.

Chantilly clapped with her petite, chubby hands. "That was a good one! The best one I've seen all week! I love it when they don't go as planned."

The officiant said, "I present to you, Ms. Chantilly and Mr. King, Mr. and Mrs. Travis Maddox."

Elvis clapped, too, and Travis lifted me in his arms. I took each side of his face into my hands and leaned over to kiss him.

"I'm just trying not to have a Tom Cruise moment," Travis said, beaming at everyone in the room. "I now understand the whole jumping on the couch and punching the floor thing. I don't know how to express how I feel! Where's Oprah?"

I let out an uncharacteristic cackle. He was grinning ear to ear, and I'm sure I looked just as annoyingly happy. Travis set me down, and then glanced around at everyone in the room.

He seemed a little shocked. "Woo!" he yelled, his fists shaking in front of him. He was having a *very* Tom Cruise moment. He laughed, and then he kissed me again. "We did it!"

I laughed with him. He took me into his arms, and I noticed that his eyes were a little glossy.

"She married me!" he said to Elvis. "I fucking love you, baby!" he yelled again, hugging and kissing me.

I wasn't sure what I expected, but this definitely wasn't it. Chantilly, the officiant, and even Elvis were laughing, half in amusement, half in awe. The photographer's flash was going off like we were surrounded by paparazzi.

"Just a few papers to sign, a few pictures, and then

you can start your happily-ever-after," Chantilly said. She turned and then faced us again with a wide, toothy grin, holding up a piece of paper and a pen.

"Oh!" Chantilly said. "Your bouquet. We're going to need that in the pictures."

She handed me the flowers, and Travis and I posed. We stood together. We showed off our rings. Side by side, face-to-face, jumping in the air, hugging, kissing—at one point Travis held me up in his arms. After a quick signing of the marriage certificate, Travis led me by the hand to the limo waiting for us outside.

"Did that really just happen?" I asked.

"It sure as hell did!"

"Did I see some misty eyes back there?"

"Pigeon, you are now Mrs. Travis Maddox. I've never been this happy in my life!"

A smile burst across my face, and I laughed and shook my head. I'd never seen a crazy person be so endearing. I lunged at him, pressing his lips against mine. Since his tongue had been in my mouth in the chapel, all I could think about was getting it back there.

Travis knotted his fingers in my hair as I climbed on top of him, and I dug my knees into the leather seat on each side of his hips. My fingers fumbled with his belt while he leaned over to press the button to lift the privacy window.

I cussed his shirt buttons for taking so long to undo,

and then began working impatiently on his zipper. Travis's mouth was everywhere; kissing the tender parts of skin just behind my ear, running his tongue down the line of my neck, and nibbling my collarbone. With one motion, he turned me onto my back, immediately sliding his hand up my thigh and hooking my panties with his finger. Within moments, they were hanging off one of my ankles, and Travis's hand was moving up the inside of my leg until he paused at the tender skin between my thighs.

"Baby," I whispered before he silenced me with his mouth. He was breathing hard through his nose, holding me against him like it was the first and the last time.

Travis pulled back onto his knees, his ripped abs and chest, and his tattoos on full display. My thighs instinctively tensed, but he took my right leg in both of his hands, gently moving them apart. I watched as his mouth hungrily worked from my toes, to my heel, my calf, my knee, and then to my inner thigh. I lifted my hips to his mouth, but he lingered on my upper legs for several moments, far more patient than I was.

Once his tongue touched the most sensitive parts of me, his fingers slid between my dress and the seat, gripping my ass, lightly tugging me toward him. Every nerve melted and tensed at the same time. Travis had been in that position before, but he had clearly been holding back; saving his best work for our wedding night. My knees bent, shook, and I grabbed at his ears.

He paused once, only to whisper my name against my wet skin, and I faltered, closing my eyes and feeling as if they were rolling to the back of my head in pure ecstasy. I moaned, making his kisses more eager, and then he tensed, lifting my body closer to his mouth.

Every passing second became more intense, a brick wall between wanting to let go and needing to stay in that moment. Finally, when I couldn't wait any longer, I reached up and buried Travis's face into me. I cried out, feeling him smiling, overcome by the intense jolts of electricity bolting throughout my body.

With all of Travis's distractions, I didn't realize we were at the Bellagio until I heard the driver's voice over the speaker. "I'm sorry, Mr. and Mrs. Maddox, but we've arrived at your hotel. Would you like me to take another drive down the Strip?"

CHAPTER EIGHT

Finally

Travis

"No, just give us a minute," I said.

Abby was half-lying, half sitting on the black leather seat of the limo, her cheeks flushed, breathing hard. I kissed her ankle, and then pulled her panties off the toe of her high heel, handing them to her.

God damn, she was a beautiful sight. I couldn't take my eyes off of her while I buttoned up my shirt. Abby flashed me a huge grin while she shimmied her panties back over her hips. The limo driver knocked on the door. Abby nodded and I gave him the green light to open it. I handed him a large bill, and then lifted my wife into my arms. We made it through the lobby and then the casino in just a few minutes. You might say I was a little motivated to get back to the room—luckily having Abby in my arms provided cover for my bulging dick.

She ignored the dozens of people staring at us while we

entered the elevator, and then planted her mouth on mine. The floor number was muffled when I tried to say it to the amused couple closest to the buttons, but I saw out of the corner of my eye that they'd pushed the right one.

As soon as we stepped into the hall, my heart began to pound. When we reached the door, I struggled with keeping Abby in my arms and getting the keycard out of my pocket.

"I'll get it, baby," she said, pulling it out and then kissing me while she unlocked the door.

"Thank you, Mrs. Maddox."

Abby smiled against my mouth. "My pleasure."

I carried her into the room and lowered her down to stand at the foot of the bed. Abby watched me for a moment while she kicked off her heels. "Let's get this out of the way, Mrs. Maddox. This is one article of clothing of yours that I don't want to ruin."

I turned her around and then slowly unzipped her dress, kissing each piece of skin as it was exposed. Every inch of Abby was already ingrained in my mind, but touching and tasting the skin of the woman that was now my wife made it new all over again. I felt an excitement I'd never felt before.

The dress fell to the floor, and I picked it up, tossing it over the back of a chair. Abby unsnapped the back of her bra, letting it fall to the floor, and I tucked my thumbs between her skin and the lacey fabric of her panties. I grinned. I'd already had them off once.

I leaned down to kiss the skin behind her ear. "I love you so much," I whispered, slowly pushing her panties down her thighs. They fell to her ankles, and she kicked them away with her bare feet. I wrapped my arms around her, taking a deep breath in through my nose, pulling her bare back against my chest. I needed to be inside her, my dick was practically reaching out for her, but it was important to take our time. We only got one shot at a wedding night, and I wanted it to be perfect.

Abby

Goose bumps formed all over my body. Four months earlier, Travis had taken something from me I'd never given to any other man. I was so hell-bent on giving it to him, I didn't have time to be nervous. Now, on our wedding night, knowing what to expect and knowing how much he loved me, I was more nervous than I had been that first night.

"Let's get this out of the way, Mrs. Maddox. This is one article of clothing of yours that I don't want to ruin," he said.

I breathed out a small laugh, remembering my buttoned-up, pink cardigan, and the pattern of blood spatters down the middle of it. Then I thought about seeing Travis in the cafeteria the first time.

"*I ruin a lot of sweaters,*" he'd said with his killer smile and dimples. The same smile I wanted to hate; the same lips that were making their way down my back right now.

Travis moved me forward, and I crawled onto the bed, looking behind me, waiting, hoping he would climb on. He was watching me, pulling off his shirt, kicking off his shoes, and dropping his slacks to the floor. He shook his head, turned me onto my back, and then settled on top of me.

"No?" I asked.

"I'd rather look into my wife's eyes than be creative . . . at least for tonight."

He brushed a loose hair from my face, and then kissed my nose. It was a little amusing watching Travis take his time, pondering how and what he wanted to do to me. Once we were naked and settled under the sheets, he took a deep breath.

"Mrs. Maddox?"

I smiled. "Yes?"

"Nothing. I just wanted to call you that."

"Good. I kind of like it."

Travis's eyes scanned my face. "Do you?"

"Is that a real question? Because it's kind of hard to show it more than taking vows to be with you forever."

Travis paused, confliction darkening his expression. "I saw you," he said, his voice barely a whisper. "In the casino."

My memory instantly went into rewind, already sure he had crossed paths with Jesse, and he'd possibly seen a woman with him who resembled me. Jealous eyes play tricks on people. Just when I was ready to argue that I hadn't seen my ex, Travis began again.

"On the floor. I saw you, Pidge."

My stomach sank. He'd seen me crying. How would I possibly explain that away? I couldn't. The only way was to create a diversion.

I pushed my head back into the pillow, looking straight into the eyes. "Why do you call me Pigeon? I mean *really*?"

My question seemed to take him off guard. I waited, hoping he would forget all about the previous topic. I didn't want to lie to his face, or admit what I'd done. Not tonight. Not ever.

His choice to allow me to change the subject was clear in his eyes. He knew what I was doing, and he was going to let me do it. "You know what a pigeon is?"

I shook my head in a tiny movement.

"It's a dove. They're really fucking smart. They're loyal, and they mate for life. That first time I saw you, in the Circle, I knew what you were. Under the buttoned-up cardigan and the blood, you weren't going to fall for my shit. You were going to make me earn it. You would require a reason to trust me. I saw it in your eyes, and I couldn't shake it until I saw you that day in the cafeteria. Even though I tried to ignore it, I knew it even then. Every fuckup, every bad choice, were bread crumbs, so that we found our way to each other. So that we found our way to this moment."

My breath faltered. "I am so in love with you."

His body was lying between my open legs, and I could feel him against my thighs, only a couple of inches from where I wanted him to be.

"You're my wife." When he said the words, a peace filled his eyes. It reminded me of the night he won the bet for me to stay at his apartment.

"Yes. You're stuck with me, now."

He kissed my chin. "Finally."

He took his time as he gently slid inside of me, closing his eyes for only a second before gazing into mine again. He rocked against me slowly, rhythmically, kissing my mouth intermittently. Even though Travis had always been careful and gentle with me, the first few moments were a little uncomfortable. He must have known that I was new to this, even though I'd never mentioned it. The whole campus knew about Travis's conquests, but my experiences with him were never the wild romps everyone talked about. Travis was always soft and tender with me; patient. Tonight was no exception. Maybe even more so.

Once I relaxed, and moved back against him, Travis reached down. He hooked his hand behind my knee and pulled up gently, stopping at his hip. He slid into me again, this time deeper. I sighed, and lifted my hip to him. There were much worse things in life than promising to feel Travis Maddox's naked body against and inside of mine for the rest of my life. Much, much worse.

He kissed me, and tasted me, and hummed against my mouth. Rocking against me, craving me, pulling at my skin as he lifted my other leg and pushed my knees against my chest so he could press himself into me even deeper. I moaned and shifted, unable to keep quiet while he positioned himself so he was entering me at different angles, working his hips until my nails were digging into the skin of his back. My fingertips were buried deep into his sweaty skin, but I could still feel his muscles bulging and sliding beneath them.

Travis's thighs were rubbing and bumping against my backside. He held himself up on one elbow, and then sat up, pulling my legs with him until my ankles were resting on his shoulders. He made love to me harder, then, and even though it was a little painful, that pain shot sparks of adrenaline all over my body. It took every bit of pleasure I was already feeling to a new level.

"Oh, God . . . Travis," I said, breathing his name. I needed to say something, anything to let go of the intensity building up inside me.

My words made his body tense, and the rhythm of his movements became faster, more rigid, until beads of sweat formed on our skin, making it easier to slide against each other.

He let my legs fall back to the bed as he positioned himself directly over me again. He shook his head. "You feel so good," he moaned. "I wanna make this last all night, but I . . ."

I touched my lips to his ear. "I want you to come," I said, ending the simple sentence with a soft, small kiss.

I relaxed my hips, letting my knees fall even farther apart and closer to the bed. Travis pressed deep inside me, over and over, his movements building as he groaned. I gripped my knee, pulling it toward my chest. The pain felt so good it was addictive, and I felt it build until my whole body tensed in short but strong bursts. I moaned loudly, not caring who might hear.

Travis groaned in reaction. Finally, his movements slowed, but they were stronger, until he finally called out. "Oh, fuck! Damn! *Agh*!" he yelled. His body twitched and trembled as he pressed his forehead hard against my cheek.

Both out of breath, we didn't speak. Travis kept his cheek against mine, twitching one more time before burying his face in the pillow under my head.

I kissed his neck, tasting the salt on his skin.

"You were right," I said.

Travis pulled back to look at me, curious.

"You were my last first kiss."

He smiled, pressed his lips against me hard, and then buried his face against my neck. He was breathing heavily but still managed to sweetly whisper, "I fucking love you, Pigeon."

CHAPTER NINE

Before

Abby

A buzzing pulled me out of a deep sleep. The curtains kept out all but the slivers of sun bordering them. The blanket and sheets were hanging halfway off our king-size bed. My dress had fallen off the chair onto the floor, joining Travis's suit that was scattered all over the room, and I could only see one of my high heels.

My naked body was tangled with Travis's, after the third time we consummated our marriage we passed out from sheer exhaustion.

Again with the buzzing. It was my phone on the night-stand. I reached over Travis and flipped it over, seeing Trent's name.

Adam arrested.

John Savage on the list of dead.

That was all he said. I felt sick as I deleted the messages, worried that maybe Trent didn't offer more because the police were at Jim's now, maybe even telling their dad that Travis might be involved. I glanced at the time on my phone. It was ten o'clock.

John Savage was one less person to investigate. One more death for Travis to feel guilty about. I tried to remember if I'd seen John after the fire broke out. He was knocked out. Maybe he'd never gotten up. I thought of those frightened girls Trent and I saw in the hall of the basement. I thought about Hilary Short, who I knew from calc class, and was smiling as she stood next to her new boyfriend near the opposite wall of Keaton Hall five minutes before the fire. How long the list of the dead really was and who was on it was something I'd tried *not* to think about.

Maybe we should all be punished. The truth was, we were all responsible, because we were all irresponsible. There is a reason why fire marshals clear these kinds of events and safety precautions are taken. We ignored all of that. Turning on a radio or the television without seeing the images on the news was impossible, so Travis and I avoided them when possible. But all this media attention meant investigators would be all the more motivated to find someone to blame. I wondered if their hunt would stop with Adam, or if they were out for blood. If I were a parent of one of those dead students, I might be.

I didn't want to see Travis go to jail for everyone's ir-responsible behavior, and right or wrong, that wouldn't bring anyone back. I had done everything I could think of to keep him out of trouble, and I would deny his presence in Keaton Hall that night to my dying breath.

People had done worse for those they loved.

"Travis," I said, nudging him. He was facedown with his head buried under a pillow.

Ugggggghhhhh, he groaned. "You want me to make breakfast? You want eggs?"

"It's just after ten."

"Still qualifies as brunch." When I didn't respond, he offered again. "Okay, an egg sandwich?"

I paused, and then looked over at him with a smile. "Baby?"

"Yeah?"

"We're in Vegas."

Travis's head popped up and he flipped on the lamp. Once the last twenty-four hours finally set in, his hand emerged from under his pillow and he hooked his arm around me, pulling me beneath him. He nestled his hips between my thighs, and then bent his head down to kiss me; softly, tenderly, letting his lips linger on mine until they were warm and tingly

"I can still get you eggs. Want me to call room service?"

"We actually have a plane to catch."

His face fell. "How much time do we have?"

"Our flight is at four. Checkout is at eleven."

Travis frowned, and looked over at the window. "I should have booked an extra day. We should be lying in bed or by the pool."

I kissed his cheek. "We have classes tomorrow. We'll save up and go somewhere later. I don't want to spend our honeymoon in Vegas, anyway."

His face screwed into disgust. "I definitely don't wanna spend it in Illinois."

I conceded with a nod. Couldn't exactly argue that. Illinois wasn't the first place that came to mind when I thought *honeymoon*. "St. Thomas is beautiful. We don't even need passports."

"That's good. Since I'm not fighting anymore, we'll need to save where we can."

I smiled. "You're not?"

"I told you, Pidge. I don't need all that when I have you. You've changed everything. You're tomorrow. You're the apocalypse."

My nose wrinkled. "I don't think I like that word."

He smiled and rolled onto the bed, just a few inches from my left side. Lying on his stomach, he pulled his hands under him, settling them under his chest, and he lay his cheek against the mattress, watching me for a moment, his eyes staring into mine.

"You said something at the wedding . . . that we were like Johnny and June. I didn't quite get the reference."

He smirked. "You don't know about Johnny Cash and June Carter?"

"Sort of."

"She fought him tooth and nail, too. They fought, and he was stupid about a lot of stuff. They worked it out and spent the rest of their lives together."

"Oh yeah? I bet she didn't have Mick for a dad."

"He'll never hurt you again, Pigeon."

"You can't promise that. Just when I start settling in somewhere, he shows up."

"Well, we're going to have regular jobs, broke like every other college student, so he won't have a reason to sniff around us for money. We'll need every dime. Good thing I still have a little left in savings to carry us through."

"Any ideas where you'll apply for a job? I thought about tutoring. Math."

Travis smiled. "You'll be good at that. Maybe I'll tutor science."

"You're very good at that. I can be a reference."

"I don't think it'll count coming from my wife."

I blinked. "Oh my God. That just sounds crazy."

Travis laughed. "Doesn't it? I fucking love it. I'm going to take care of you, Pidge. I can't promise that Mick will never hurt you again, but I can promise that I'll do everything I can to keep that from happening. And if it does, I'll love you through it."

I offered a small smile, and then reached up to touch his cheek. "I love you."

"I love you," he said right back. "Was he a good dad . . . before all that?"

"I don't know," I said, looking up at the ceiling. "I guess I thought he was. But what does a kid know about being a good parent? I have good memories of him. He drank for as long as I can remember, and gambled, but when his luck was up, he was kind. Generous. A lot of his friends were family men . . . they also worked for the mob, but they had kids. They were nice and didn't mind Mick bringing me around. I spent a lot of time behind the scenes, seeing things most kids don't get to see because he took me everywhere then." I felt a smile creep up, and then a tear fell. "Yeah, I guess he was, in his own way. I loved him. To me, he was perfect."

Travis touched his fingertip to my temple, tenderly wiping the moisture away. "Don't cry, Pidge."

I shook my head, trying to play it off. "See? He can still hurt me, even when he's not here."

"I'm here," he said, taking my hand in his. He was still staring at me, his cheek against the sheets. "You turned my world upside down, and I got a brand-new beginning . . . like an apocalypse."

I frowned. "I still don't like it."

He pushed off the bed, wrapping the sheet around his waist. "It depends on how you look at it."

"No, not really," I said, watching him walk to the bathroom.

"I'll be out in five."

I stretched, letting all of my limbs spread in every direction on the bed, and then I sat up, combing my hair out with my fingers. The toilet flushed, and then the faucet turned on. He wasn't kidding. He would be ready in a few minutes and I was still naked in bed.

Fitting my dress and his suit in the carry-on proved to be a challenge, but I finally made it work. Travis emerged from the bathroom and brushed his fingers across mine as we passed.

Teeth brushed, hair combed, I changed and we were checking out by eleven.

Travis took pictures of the lobby ceiling with his phone, and then we took one last look around before leaving for the long taxi line. Even in the shade it was hot, and my legs were already sticking to my jeans.

My phone buzzed in my purse. I checked it quickly.

Cops just left. Dad's @ Tim's but I told them you guys were in Vegas getting married. I think they fucking bought it.

Srsly?

Yeah! I should get an Oscar for that shit. JS

I breathed a long sigh of relief.

"Who's that?" Travis asked.

"America," I said, letting the phone slip back into my purse. "She's pissed."

He smiled. "I bet."

"Where to? The airport?" Travis asked, holding his hand out for mine.

I took it, turning it enough so that I could see my nickname on his wrist. "No, I'm thinking we need to make a pit stop first."

One of his eyebrows pulled up. "To where?"

"You'll see."

CHAPTER TEN

Inked

Abby

"What do you mean?" Travis said, blanching. "We're not here for me?"

The tattoo artist stared at us both, a little surprised at Travis's surprise.

The entire taxi ride over, Travis assumed I was buying him a new tattoo as a wedding present. When I told the driver our destination, it never occurred to Travis that I would be the one getting inked. He talked about tattooing ABBY somewhere on him, but since he already had PIGEON on his wrist, I thought it would be redundant.

"It's my turn," I said, turning to the tattoo artist. "What's your name?"

"Griffin," he said in a monotone.

"Of course," I said. "I want MRS. MADDOX here." I touched my finger to my jeans on the right side of my lower abdomen, just low enough not to be seen, even in a bikini. I wanted Travis to be the only one privy to my ink, a nice surprise every time he undressed me.

Travis beamed. "Mrs. Maddox?"

"Yes, in this font," I said, pointing to a laminated poster on the wall featuring sample tattoos.

Travis smiled. "That fits you. It's elegant, but not fussy."

"Exactly. Can you do that?"

"I can. It'll be about an hour. We have a couple people ahead of you. It'll be two fifty."

"Two fifty? For a few scribbles?" Travis said, his mouth falling open. "What the fuck, chuck?"

"It's Griffin," he said, unaffected.

"I know, but—"

"It's okay, baby," I said. "Everything is more in Vegas."

"Let's just wait until we get home, Pidge."

"Pidge?" Griffin said.

Travis sent him a death glare. "Shut up," he warned, looking back at me. "This'll be two hundred bucks cheaper back home."

"If I wait, I won't do it."

Griffin shrugged. "Then maybe you should wait."

I glared at Travis and Griffin. "I'm not waiting. I'm doing this." I pulled out my wallet and shoved three bills at Griffin. "So you take my money"—I frowned at Travis—"and you hush. It's my money, my body, and this is what I want to do."

Travis seemed to weigh what he was about to say. "But . . . it's going to hurt."

I smiled. "Me? Or you?"

"Both."

Griffin took my money and then disappeared. Travis paced the floor like a nervous expectant father. He peeked down the hall, and then paced some more. It was as cute as it was annoying. At one point he begged me not to do it, and then became impressed and touched that I was so hell-bent on going through with it.

"Pull down your jeans," Griffin said, getting his equipment ready.

Travis shot a piercing look at the short, muscular man from under his brow, but Griffin was too busy to notice Travis's most frightening expression.

I sat on the chair, and Griffin pushed buttons. As the chair reclined, Travis sat on a stool on the other side of me. He was fidgeting.

"Trav," I said in a soft voice. "Sit down." I held out my hand and he took it, also taking a seat. He kissed my fingers, and offered a sweet but nervous smile.

Just when I thought he couldn't take the waiting anymore, my cell phone buzzed in my purse.

Oh, God. What if it was a text message from Trent? Travis was already digging for it, grateful for the distraction.

"Leave it, Trav."

He looked at the display and frowned. My breath caught. He held out the phone for me to take. "It's Mare."

I grabbed it from him and would've felt relief if it

101

weren't for the cold cotton swab running over my hip bone. "Hello?"

"Abby?" America said. "Where are you? Shepley and I just got home. The car is gone."

"Oh," I said, my voice an octave higher. I hadn't planned on telling her yet. I wasn't sure how to break the news, but I was sure she was going to hate me. At least for a little while.

"We're . . . in Vegas."

America laughed. "Shut up."

"I'm totally serious."

America grew quiet, and then her voice was so loud, I flinched. "WHY are you in Vegas? It's not like you had a good time when you were there last!"

"Travis and I decided to . . . we kind of got married, Mare."

"What! This isn't funny, Abby! You better be fucking joking!"

Griffin placed the transfer onto my skin and pressed. Travis looked like he wanted to kill him for touching me.

"You're silly," I said, but when the tattoo machine began to hum my entire body tensed.

"What's that noise?" America said, steaming.

"We're at the tattoo parlor."

"Is Travis getting branded with your real name this time?"

"Not exactly . . ."

Travis was sweating. "Baby . . ." he said, frowning.

"I can do this," I said, focusing on spots on the ceiling. I jumped when Griffin's fingertip's touched my skin, but I tried not to tense.

"Pigeon," Travis said, his voice tinged with desperation.

"All right," I said, shaking my head dismissively. "I'm ready." I held the phone away from my ear, wincing from both the pain, and the inevitable lecture.

"I'm going to kill you, Abby Abernathy!" America cried. "Kill you!"

"Technically, it's Abby Maddox, now," I said, smiling at Travis.

"It's not fair!" she whined. "I was supposed to be your maid of honor! I was supposed to go dress shopping with you and throw a bachelorette party and hold your bouquet!"

"I know," I said, watching Travis's smile fade as I winced again.

"You don't have to do this, you know," he said, his eyebrow pulling together.

I squeezed his fingers. "I know."

"You said that already!" America snapped.

"I wasn't talking to you."

"Oh, you're talking to me," she fumed. "You are soooo talking to me. You are never going to hear the end of this, do you hear me? I will never, ever forgive you!"

"Yes you will."

"You! You're a . . . ! You're just plain mean, Abby! You're a horrible best friend!"

I laughed, causing Griffin to pull back. He breathed through his nose.

"I'm sorry," I said.

"Who was that?" America snapped.

"That was Griffin," I answered matter-of-factly.

"Is she done?" he asked Travis, annoyed.

Travis nodded once. "Keep it up."

Griffin just smiled, and continued. My whole body tensed again.

"Who the hell is Griffin? Let me guess: you invited a total stranger to your wedding and not your best friend?"

I cringed, from both her shrill voice and the needle stabbing into my skin. "No. He didn't go to the wedding," I said, sucking in a breath of air.

Travis sighed and shifted nervously in his chair, squeezing my hand. He looked miserable. I couldn't help but smile.

"I'm supposed to be squeezing your hand, remember?"

"Sorry," he said, his voice thick with distress. "I don't think I can take this." He opened his hand a bit and looked to Griffin.

"Hurry up, would ya?"

Griffin shook his head. "Covered in tats and can't take

your girlfriend getting a simple script. I'll be finished in a minute, mate."

Travis's expression turned severe. "Wife. She's my wife."

America gasped, the sound as high-pitched as her tone. "You're getting a tattoo? What is going on with you, Abby? Did you breathe toxic fumes in that fire?"

"Travis has my name on his wrist," I said, looking down at the smeared, black mess on my stomach. Griffin pressed the tip of the needle against my skin, and I clenched my teeth together. "We're married," I said through my teeth. "I wanted something, too."

Travis shook his head. "You didn't have to."

I narrowed my eyes. "Don't start with me."

The corners of his mouth turned up, and he gazed at me with the sweetest adoration I'd ever seen.

America laughed, sounding a bit insane. "You've gone crazy." *She should talk.* "I'm committing you to the asylum when I get home."

"It's not that crazy. We love each other. We have been practically living together on and off all year." *Okay, not quite all year . . . not that it matters now. Not enough to mention it and give America more ammunition.*

"Because you're nineteen, you idiot! Because you ran off and didn't tell anyone, and because I'm not there!" she cried.

For one second, guilt and second thoughts crept in. For one second, I let the tiniest bit of panic that I'd just made a huge mistake simmer to the surface, but the moment I looked up at Travis and saw the incredible amount of love in his eyes, it all went away.

"I'm sorry, Mare, I have to go. I'll see you tomorrow, okay?"

"I don't know if I want to see you tomorrow! I don't think I want to see Travis ever again!"

"I'll see you tomorrow, Mare. I know you want to see my ring."

"And your tat," she said, a smile in her voice.

I handed the phone to Travis. Griffin ran his thousand tiny knives of pain and anguish across my angry skin again. Travis shoved my phone in his pocket, gripping my hand with both of his, leaning down to touch his forehead to mine.

Not knowing what to expect helped, but the pain was a slow burn. As Griffin filled in the thicker parts of the letters I winced, and every time he pulled away to wipe the excess ink away with a cloth, I relaxed.

After a few more complaints from Travis, Griffin made us jump with a loud proclamation. "DONE!"

"Thank God!" I said, letting my head fall back against the chair.

"Thank God!" Travis cried, and then sighed in relief. He patted my hand, smiling.

I looked down, admiring the beautiful black lines hiding under the smeared black mess.

Mrs. Maddox

"Wow," I said, rising up on my elbows.

Travis's frown instantly turned into a triumphant smile. "It's beautiful."

Griffin shook his head. "If I had a dollar for every inked-up new husband who brought his wife in here and took it worse than she did—well, I wouldn't have to tat anyone ever again."

Travis's smile disappeared. "Just give her the postcare instructions, smart-ass."

"I'll have a printout of instructions and some A and D ointment at the counter," Griffin said, amused by Travis.

My stare kept returning to the elegant script on my skin. We were married. I was a Maddox, just like all of those wonderful men I had grown to love. I had a family, albeit full of angry, crazy, lovable men, but they were mine. I belonged to them, as they belonged to me.

Travis held out his hand, peering down at his ring finger. "We did it, baby. I still can't believe you're my wife."

"Believe it." I beamed.

I reached out to Travis, pointed to his pocket, and then turned my hand over, opening my palm. He handed me my phone, and I pulled up the camera to snap a picture of my fresh ink. Travis helped me from the chair, careful to avoid my right side. I was sensitive to every movement that caused my jeans to rub against my raw skin.

After a short stop at the front counter, Travis let go of me long enough to push the door open for me, and then we walked outside to a waiting cab. My cell phone rang again. America.

"She's going to lay on the guilt trip thick, isn't she?" Travis said, watching me silence my phone. I wasn't in the mood to endure another tongue-lashing.

"She'll pout for twenty-four hours after she sees the pictures—then she'll get over it."

"Are you sure about that, Mrs. Maddox?"

I chuckled. "Are you ever going to stop calling me that? You've said it a hundred times since we left the chapel."

He shook his head as he held the cab door open for me. "I'll quit calling you that when it sinks in that this is real."

"Oh, it's real all right. I have wedding night memories to prove it." I slid to the middle and then watched as he slid in next to me.

He leaned against me, running his nose up the sensitive skin of my neck until he reached my ear. "We sure do."

CHAPTER ELEVEN

The Road Home

Travis

Abby watched Las Vegas pass by her window. Just the sight of her made me want to touch her, and now that she was my wife, that feeling was amplified. But I was trying very hard not to make her regret her decision. Playing it cool used to be my superpower. Now I was dangerously close to being Shepley.

Unable to stop myself, I slid my hand over and barely touched her pinky finger. "I saw pictures of my parents' wedding. I thought Mom was the most beautiful bride I'd ever see. Then I saw you at the chapel, and I changed my mind."

She looked down at our fingers touching, intertwined her fingers in mine, and then looked up at me. "When you say things like that, Travis, it makes me fall in love with you all over again." She nuzzled up against me, and then kissed my cheek. "I wish I could have known her."

"Me, too." I paused, wondering if I should say the thought that was in my head. "What about your mom?"

Abby shook her head, leaning into my arms. "She wasn't all that great before we moved to Wichita. After we got there, her depression got worse. She just checked out. If I hadn't met America, I would have been alone."

She was already in my arms, but I wanted to hug my wife's sixteen-year-old self, too. And her childhood self, for that matter. There was so much that had happened to her that I couldn't protect her from.

"I . . . I know it's not true, but Mick told me so many times that I ruined him. Both of them. I have this irrational fear that I'll do the same to you."

"Pigeon," I scolded, kissing her hair.

"It's weird though, right? That when I started playing, his luck went south. He said I took his luck. Like I had that power over him. It made for some seriously conflicting emotions for a teenage girl."

The hurt in her eyes caused a familiar fire to come over me, but I quickly doused the flames with a deep breath. I wasn't sure if seeing Abby hurt would ever make me feel anything less than a little crazy, but she didn't need a hotheaded boyfriend. She needed an understanding husband. "If he had any fucking sense, he would have made you his lucky charm instead of his enemy. It really is his loss, Pidge. You're the most amazing woman I know."

She picked at her nails. "He didn't want me to be his luck."

"You could be my luck. I'm feeling pretty fucking lucky right now."

She playfully elbowed me in the ribs. "Let's just keep it that way."

"I have not a single doubt that we will. You don't know it yet, but you just saved me."

Something sparked in Abby's eyes, and she pressed her cheek against my shoulder. "I hope so."

Abby

Travis hugged me to his side, letting go just long enough for us to move forward. We weren't the only overly affectionate couple waiting in line at the check-in counter. It was the end of spring break, and the airport was packed.

Once we got our boarding passes, we made our way slowly through security. When we finally reached the front of the line, Travis kept setting off the detector, so the TSA agent made him take off his ring.

Travis grudgingly complied, but once we passed through security and sat on a nearby bench to put on our shoes, Travis grumbled a few inaudible swear words, and then relaxed.

"It's okay, baby. It's back on your finger," I said, giggling at his overreaction.

Travis didn't speak, only kissed my forehead before we left security for our gate. The other spring breakers appeared just as exhausted and happy as we were. And I spotted other arriving couples holding hands who looked just as nervous and excited as Travis and I were when we arrived in Vegas.

I grazed Travis's fingertips with mine.

He sighed.

His response caught me off guard. It was heavy, and full of stress. The closer we got to the gate, the slower he walked. I worried about the reaction we'd face at home, too, but I was more worried about the investigation. Maybe he was thinking the same thing and didn't want to talk to me about it.

At Gate Eleven, Travis sat next to me, keeping his hand in mine. His knee was bouncing, and he kept touching and tugging at his lips with his free hand. His three-day scruff twitched every time he moved his mouth. He was either freaking out on the inside, or he'd drunk a pot of coffee without me knowing.

"Pigeon?" he said finally.

Oh thank God. He's going to talk to me about it.

"Yeah?"

He thought about what he might say, and then sighed again. "Nothing."

Whatever it was, I wanted to fix it. But if he wasn't

thinking about the investigation or facing the aftermath of the fire, I didn't want to bring it up. Not long after we took our seat, first class was being called to board. Travis and I stood with everyone else to get in line for economy.

Travis shifted from one foot to the other, rubbing the back of his neck and squeezing my hand. He so obviously wanted to tell me something. It was eating at him, and I didn't know what else to do but squeeze his hand back.

When our boarding group began to form a line, Travis hesitated. "I can't shake this feeling," he said.

"What do you mean? Like a bad feeling?" I said, suddenly very nervous. I didn't know if he meant the plane, or Vegas, or going home. Everything that could go wrong between our next step and our arrival back on campus flashed through my mind.

"I have this crazy feeling that once we get home, I'm going to wake up. Like none of this was real." Concern shone in his eyes, making them glassy.

Of all the things to worry about, and he was worried about losing me, just as I worried about losing him. It was then, in that moment, that I knew we'd done the right thing. That yes, we were young, and yes, we were crazy, but we were as much in love as anyone. We were older than Romeo and Juliet. Older than my grandparents. It might not have been that long ago since we were children, but there were people with ten or more years of experience who still didn't have it together. We didn't have it all together, but we had each other, and that was more than enough.

When we returned, it was likely that everyone would be waiting for the breakdown, waiting for the deterioration of a couple married too young. Just imagining the stares and stories and whispers made my skin crawl. It might take a lifetime to prove to everyone that this works. We'd made so many mistakes, and undoubtedly we would make thousands more, but the odds were in our favor. We'd proven them all wrong before.

After a tennis match of worries and reassurances, I finally wrapped my arms around my husband's neck, touching my lips ever so slightly to his. "I'd bet my firstborn. That's how sure I am." This was a wager I wouldn't lose.

"You can't be that sure," he said.

I raised an eyebrow, my mouth pulling to the side. "Wanna bet?"

Travis relaxed, taking his boarding pass from my fingers, and handing it to the attendant.

"Thank you," she said, scanning it and then handing it back. She did the same to mine, and just as we had little more than twenty-four hours before, we walked hand in hand down the Jetway.

"Are you hinting at something?" Travis asked. He stopped. "You're not . . . is that why you wanted to get married?"

I laughed, shook my head, and pulled him along. "God, no. I think we've taken a big enough step to last us a while."

He nodded once. "Fair enough, Mrs. Maddox." He squeezed my hand, and we boarded the plane for home.

CHAPTER TWELVE

Anniversary

Abby

Water beaded on my skin, mixing with the sunscreen and magnifying the texture of my tanned stomach. The sun beat down on us, and everyone else on the beach, making the heat dance in waves on top of the sand between the patches of brightly colored beach towels.

"Ma'am," the waiter said, leaning down with two drinks. Sweat dripped off his dark skin, but he was smiling. "Charging to the room?"

"Yes, thank you," I said, taking my frozen strawberry margarita and signing the check.

America took hers and stirred the ice with her tiny straw. "This. Is. Heaven."

We all deserved a little Heaven to recover from the last year. After attending dozens of funerals, and helping Travis deal with his guilt, we fielded more questions from investigators. The students who were at the fight kept Travis's name out of it when speaking with the authorities, but rumors spread, and it took a long time for Adam's arrest to be enough for the families.

It took a lot of convincing for Travis not to turn himself in. The only thing that seemed to hold him back was my begging for him not to leave me alone, and knowing Trent would be charged with misleading an investigation. The first six months of our marriage was far from easy, and we spent a lot of long nights arguing about what was the right thing to do. Maybe it was wrong for me to keep Travis from prison, but I didn't care. I didn't believe he was any more at fault than anyone who had chosen to be in that basement that night. I would never regret my decision, just like I would never regret looking straight into that detective's eyes and lying my ass off to save my husband.

"Yes," I said, watching the water climb up the sand and then recede. "We have Travis to thank. He was at the gym with as many clients as he could fit around his classes six days a week from five in the morning to ten o'clock at night. This was all him. It sure wasn't my tutoring money that got us here."

"Thank him? When he promised me a real wedding, I didn't know he meant a year later!"

"America," I scolded, turning to her. "Could you be more spoiled? We're on a beach, drinking frozen margaritas in St. Thomas."

"I guess it gave me some time to plan your bachelorette party and the renewal of your vows," she said, taking a sip.

I smiled, turning to her. "Thank you. I mean it. And this is the best bachelorette party in the history of bachelorette parties."

Harmony walked over and sat down in the lounge chair on the other side of me, her pixie short chestnut hair glistened in the sun. She shook the salt water out of it, making it feather out. "The water is so warm!" she said, pushing up her oversize sunglasses. "There is a guy over there teaching kids how to windsurf. He's stupid hot."

"Maybe you can talk him into being our stripper later?" America said, straight-faced.

Kara frowned. "America, no. Travis would be livid. Abby isn't *actually* a bachelorette, remember?"

America shrugged, letting her eyes close behind her sunglasses. Although Kara and I had grown very close since I moved out, she and America still weren't on the best of terms. Probably because both of them said exactly what they thought.

"We'll blame it on Harmony," America said. "Travis can't get mad at her. He's forever indebted to her for letting him into Morgan Hall that night you were fighting."

"Doesn't mean I want to be on the wrong end of a Maddox rage," Harmony said, shuddering.

I scoffed. "You know he hasn't lashed out in a long time. He's got a handle on his anger now."

Harmony and I had shared two classes that semester, and when I invited her to the apartment to study, Travis recognized her as the girl who'd let him into our dorm. Like Travis, her brother was also a member of Sigma Tau fraternity, so she was one of the few pretty girls on campus that Travis hadn't slept with.

"Travis and Shepley will be here tomorrow afternoon," America said. "We have to get our partying in tonight. You don't think Travis is sitting at home doing nothing, do you? We're going out and we're going to have a damn good time whether you like it or not."

"That's fine," I said. "Just no strippers. And not too late. This wedding will actually have an audience. I don't want to look hungover."

Harmony lifted the flag next to her chair, and almost immediately a waiter came over.

"How may I help you, miss?"

"A piña colada, please?"

"Of course," he said, backing away.

"This place is swank," America said.

"And you wonder why it took us a year to save up for this."

"You're right. I shouldn't have said anything. Trav wanted you to have the best. I get it. And it was nice of Mom and Dad to pay my way. I sure as hell wouldn't have been able to come otherwise."

I giggled.

"You promised me I could be a bridesmaid and do everything you made me miss last year. I see them paying as a wedding present and an anniversary present to you, and a birthday present to me all rolled into one. If you ask me, they got off cheap."

"It's still too much."

"Abby, they love you like a daughter. Daddy is very excited about walking you down the aisle. Let them do this without ruining the spirit of it," America said.

I smiled. Mark and Pam treated me like family. After my father landed me in a dangerous situation last year, Mark decided that I needed a new father—and nominated himself. If I needed help with tuition or books or a new vacuum cleaner, Mark and Pam showed up at my door. Helping me also gave them an excuse to visit America and me, and it was obvious that they enjoyed that the most.

Not only did I now have the unruly Maddox clan as family, but I had Mark and Pam as well. I'd gone from belonging to no one, to being a part of two amazing families that were incredibly important to me. At first, it made me feel anxious. I'd never had so much to lose before. But over time, I realized that my new family wasn't going anywhere, and I learned how much good could come from misfortune.

"Sorry. I'll try to just accept this graciously."

"Thank you."

"Thank you!" Harmony said, taking her drink from the tray. She signed the bill and began sipping the fruity concoction. "I'm just so excited to be going to this one!"

"Me, too," America said, glaring in my direction. She had barely forgiven me for getting married without her. And, honestly, I hoped she'd never try to pull the same move on me. But marriage was still a long way off for her.

She and Shepley were going to get their own apartment, but both decided that even though they were always around each other, America would stay in Morgan, and Shepley would move into Helms, a men's dorm. Mark and Pam were happier about this arrangement. They loved Shepley but were worried that the stress of real-world bills and jobs would affect Shepley's and America's focus on school. America was struggling, even at the dorms.

"I just hope it goes smoothly. I hate the thought of standing in front of all those people staring at us."

America breathed out a laugh. "Elvis wasn't invited, but I'm sure it will still be beautiful."

"I still can't believe Elvis was at your wedding," Harmony said, giggling.

"Not the dead one," Kara deadpanned.

"He wasn't invited this time," I said, watching the children taking lessons celebrate windsurfing on their own.

"What was it like? Getting married in Vegas?" Harmony asked.

"It was . . ." I said, thinking about the moment we left, almost exactly a year earlier. "Stressful and frightening. I was worried. I cried. It was pretty much perfect."

Harmony's expression was one of combined disgust and surprise. "Sounds like it."

Travis

"Fuck you," I said, not amused.

"Oh, c'mon!" Shepley said, shaking with laughter. "You used to say I was the whipped one."

"Fuck you again."

Shepley turned off the ignition. He had parked the Charger on the far side of Cherry Papa's parking lot. Home of the fattest, dirtiest strippers in town. "It's not like you're going to take one of them home."

"I promised Pidge. No strippers."

"I promised you a bachelor party."

"Dude, let's just go home. I'm full, tired, and we've got a plane to catch in the morning."

Shepley frowned. "The girls have been lying on a beach in St. Thomas all day, and now they're probably partying it up in a club."

I shook my head. "We don't go to clubs without each other. She wouldn't do that."

"She would if America planned it."

I shook my head again. "No, she fucking wouldn't. I'm

not going into the strip club. Either pick something else, or take me home."

Shepley sighed, and squinted his eyes. "What about that?"

I followed his line of sight to the next block over. "A hotel? Shep, I love ya, man, but it's not a real bachelor party. I'm married. And even if I weren't, I still wouldn't have sex with you."

Shepley shook his head. "There's a bar in there. It's not a club. Is that permitted on your long list of marriage rules?"

I frowned. "I just respect my wife. And yes, douche bag, we can go in there."

"Awesome," he said, rubbing his hands together.

We walked across the street, and Shepley opened the door. It was pitch-black.

"Uh . . ." I began.

Suddenly the lights turned on. The twins, Taylor and Tyler, threw confetti in my face, music began to blare, and then I saw the worst thing I'd ever seen in my life: Trenton in a man thong, covered in about ten pounds of body glitter. He had on a cheap, yellow wig, and Cami was laughing her head off, cheering him on.

Shepley pushed me in the rest of the way. My dad was on one side of the room, standing next to Thomas. They were both shaking their heads. My uncle Jack was on the other side of Thomas, and then the rest of the room was filled with Sigma Tau brothers and football players.

"I said no strippers," I said, watching dumbfounded as Trenton danced around the room to Britney Spears.

Shepley burst into laughter. "I know, brother, but looks like the stripping happened before we got here."

It was a train wreck. My face screwed into disgust as I watched Trenton bump and grind his way across the room—even though I didn't want to. Everyone in the room was cheering him on. Cardboard cutouts of tits were hanging from the ceiling, and there was even a booby cake on a table next to my dad. I'd been to several bachelor parties before, and this one had to win some sort of a freak prize.

"Hey," Trenton said, breathless and sweaty. He pulled a few yellow strands of fake hair from his face.

"Did you lose a bet?" I asked.

"As a matter of fact, I did."

Taylor and Tyler were across the room, slapping their knees and laughing so hard they could barely breathe.

I slapped Trenton's ass. "You look hot, bro."

"Thanks," he said. The music started and he shook his hips at me. I pushed him away, and, undeterred, he danced across the room to entertain the crowd.

I looked at Shepley. "I can't wait to watch you explain this to Abby."

He smiled. "She's your wife. You do it."

For the next four hours, we drank, and talked, and watched Trenton make a complete ass out of himself. My dad, as expected, cut out early. He, along with my other brothers, had a plane to catch. We were all flying to St. Thomas in the morning for the renewal of my vows.

For the last year, Abby tutored, and I did some personal training at the local gym. We'd managed to save a little after school costs, rent, and the car payment to fly to St. Thomas and stay a few days in a nice hotel. We had plenty of things the money could have gone to, but America kept talking about it and wouldn't let us drop the idea. Then when America's parents presented us with the wedding gift/America's birthday present/anniversary gift, we tried to say no, but America was insistent.

"All right, boys. I'm going to be hurtin' in the morning if I don't call it a night."

Everyone groaned and taunted me with words like *whipped* and *pussy*, but the truth was they were all used to the new, tamer Travis Maddox. I hadn't put my fist to someone's face in almost a year.

I yawned, and Shepley punched me in the shoulder. "Let's go."

We drove in silence. I wasn't sure what Shepley was thinking about, but I couldn't fucking wait to see my wife. She'd left the day before, and that was the first time we'd been apart since we'd been married.

Shepley pulled up to the apartment and shut off the car. "Front door service, loser."

"Admit it. You miss it."

"The apartment? Yeah, a little. But I miss you fighting and us making shit tons of money more."

"Yeah. I do sometimes, too. See you in the morning."

"Pick you up right back here at six thirty."

"Later."

Shepley drove away while I slowly climbed the steps, searching for the apartment key. I hated coming home when Abby wasn't here. There was nothing worse after we met, and it was the same now. Maybe even more miserable because Shepley and America weren't even there to annoy me.

I pushed in the key and opened the door, locking it behind me and tossing my wallet onto the breakfast bar. I had already taken Toto to the pet hotel to be boarded while we were gone. It was too fucking quiet. I sighed. The apartment had changed a lot in the last year. The posters and bar signs had come down, and pictures of us and paintings went up. It was no longer a bachelor pad, but it was a good trade.

I went into my bedroom, stripped down to my Calvin Klein boxer briefs, and climbed into the bed, burying myself under the blue and green floral comforter—something else that would have never seen the inside of this apartment had Abby not had a hand in it. I pulled her pillow over and rested my head on it. It smelled like her.

The clock read 2:00 AM. I would be with her in twelve hours.

CHAPTER ~~THIRTEEN~~ FOURTEEN

Bachelorette

Abby

Those seated on the far edge of the restaurant began to scream, nearly pushing over tables and children to get away. Wineglasses broke and silverware clanged on the floor. A pineapple-shaped hurricane was knocked over, rolled off a table, and broke. America rolled her eyes at the twenty or so people gathered a few tables over. "Christ on the cross, people! It's just a little rain!"

The waitstaff and hostesses scrambled to release the rolled-up walls of the outdoor restaurant.

"And you were grumbling because we didn't have an ocean view," Harmony teased.

"Yeah, those snobby bitches aren't smirking now, are they?" America said, nodded and smiling to the six-pack of blondes now huddling and wet.

"Knock it off, Mare. You've had one too many glasses of wine," I said.

"I'm on vacation, and it's a bachelorette party. I'm supposed to be drunk."

I patted her hand. "That would be fine if you weren't a mean drunk."

"Fuck you, whore, I am *not* a mean drunk." I glared at her, and she winked at me and smiled. "Just kiddin'."

Harmony let her fork fall to her plate. "I'm stuffed. Now what?"

America pulled a small three-ring binder from her purse with a devious grin. It had small, foam letters glued to the front that read TRAVIS & ABBY and our wedding date. "Now we play a game."

"What kind of game?" I asked, wary.

She opened the binder. "Since Cami couldn't be here until tomorrow, she made you this," she said, turning the front over to read the words painted on the front. "The What Would Your Husband Say? Game. I've heard about it. Super fun, although typically it's about your *future* husband," she said, shifting excitedly in her seat. "So . . . Cami asked Travis these questions last week, and sent the book with me."

"What?" I shrieked. "What kind of questions?"

"You're getting ready to find out," she said, waving the waiter over. He brought a full tray of brightly colored Jell-O shots.

"Oh my," I said.

"If you get them wrong, you drink. If you get them right, we drink. Ready?"

"Sure," I said, glancing at Kara and Harmony.

America cleared her throat, holding the binder in front of her. "When did Travis know you were the one?"

I thought for a minute. "That first poker night at his dad's."

Errrr! America made a horrendous noise with her throat. "When he realized he wasn't good enough for you, which was the moment he saw you. Drink!"

"Aw!" Harmony said, holding her hand to her chest.

I picked up a small plastic cup and squeezed its contents into my mouth. Yum. I wasn't going to mind losing at all.

"Next question!" America said. "What is his favorite thing about you?"

"My cooking."

Errrrr! America made the noise again. "Drink!"

"You suck at this game," Kara said, clearly amused.

"Maybe I'm doing it on purpose? These are good!" I said, popping another shot into my mouth.

"Travis's answer? Your laugh."

"Wow," I said, surprised. "That's kind of endearing."

"What is his favorite part of your body?"

"My eyes."

"Ding, ding, ding! Correct!"

Harmony and Kara clapped, I bowed my head. "Thank you, thank you. Now drink, bitches."

They all laughed, and popped their shots.

America turned a page and read the next question. "When does Travis want to have kids?"

"Oh," I blew through my lips. "In seven . . . eight years?"

"A year after graduation."

Kara and Harmony made the same face, their mouths forming "oh."

"I'll drink," I said. "But he and I will have to talk about that one some more."

America shook her head. "This is a prewedding game, Abby. You should be much better at this."

"Shut up. Continue."

Kara pointed. "Technically she can't shut up and continue."

"Shut up," American and I said in unison.

"Next question!" America said. "What do you think Travis's favorite moment of your relationship was?"

"The night he won the bet and I moved in?"

"Correct again!" America said.

"This is so sweet. I can't take it," Harmony said.

"Drink! Next question," I said, smiling.

"What is one thing Travis said he'll never forget that you've said to him?"

"Wow. I have no idea."

Kara leaned in. "Just guess."

"The first time I said I loved him?"

America narrowed her eyes, thinking. "Technically,

you're wrong. He said it was the time you told Parker you loved Travis!" America burst into laughter, and so did the rest of us. "Drink!"

America turned another page. "What is the one item Travis can't live without?"

"His motorcycle."

"Correct!"

"Where was your first date?"

"Technically it was the Pizza Shack."

"Correct!" America said again.

"Ask her something more difficult, or we're going to get hammered," Kara said, throwing back another shot.

"Hmmm . . ." America said, thumbing through the pages. "Oh, here we go. What do you think Abby's favorite thing about you is?"

"What kind of question is that?" I asked. They watched me expectantly. "Um . . . my favorite thing about him is the way he always touches me when we sit together, but I bet he said his tats."

"Damn it!" America said. "Correct!" They drank, and I clapped to celebrate my small victory.

"One more," America said. "What does Travis think your favorite present from him is?"

I paused for a few seconds. "That's easy. The scrapbook he got me for Valentine's Day this year. Now, drink!"

Everyone laughed, and even though it was their turn, I shared the last shot with them.

Harmony wiped her mouth with a napkin, and helped me to collect the empty cups and place them on the tray. "What's the plan now, Mare?"

America fidgeted, clearly excited about what she was about to say. "We hit the clubs, that's what."

I shook my head. "No way. We talked about this."

America stuck out her lip.

"Don't," I said. "I'm here to renew my vows, not to get a divorce. Think of something else."

"Why doesn't he trust you?" America said, her voice very closely resembling a whine.

"If I really wanted to go, I would go. I just respect my husband, and I would rather get along than sit in a smoky club with lights that give me a headache. It would just make him wonder what went on, and I'd rather not go there. It's worked so far."

"I respect Shepley. I still go to clubs without him."

"No, you don't."

"Only because I haven't wanted to, yet. Tonight, I do."

"Well, I don't."

America's brows pulled together. "Fine. Plan B. Poker night?"

"Very funny."

Harmony's face lit up. "I saw a flyer for movie night tonight at Honeymoon Beach! They bring a screen right on the water."

America made a face. "Boring."

"No, I think it sounds fun. When does it start?"

Harmony checked her watch, and then her face fell, deflated. "In fifteen minutes."

"We can make it!" I said, grabbing my purse. "Check please!"

Travis

"Calm your tits, dude," Shepley said. He looked down at my fingers nervously beating against the metal armrest. We had landed safely and taxied in, but for whatever reason they weren't ready to let us off yet. Everyone was quietly waiting for that one, tiny *ding* that meant freedom. Something about the *ding* of the fasten seat belt light that made everyone jump up and scramble to get their carry-on luggage and stand in line. I actually had a reason to be in a hurry, though, so the wait was particularly irritating.

"What the fuck is taking so long?" I said, maybe a little too loud. A woman in front of us with a grade-school-age kid turned slowly to give me a look. "Sorry." She faced forward in a huff.

I looked down at my watch. "We're going to be late."

"No we're not," Shepley said in his typical smooth and calming voice. "We've still got plenty of time."

I stretched to the side, looking down the aisle, as if that would help. "The flight attendants haven't moved. Wait, one is on the phone."

135

"That's a good sign."

I sat upright and sighed. "We're gonna be late."

"No. We're not. You just miss her."

"I do," I said. I knew that I looked pitiful and I wasn't even going to attempt to hide it. This was the first time Abby and I had spent a night apart since before we were married, and it was miserable. Even after a year, I still looked forward to when she'd wake up in the morning. I even missed her when I slept.

Shepley shook his head in disapproval. "Remember when you used to give me so much shit for acting like this?"

"You didn't love them the way I love her."

Shepley smiled. "You really happy, man?"

"As much as I loved her back then, I love her even more, now. Like the way Dad used to talk about Mom."

Shepley smiled and then opened his mouth to respond, but the fasten seat belt light dinged, sending everyone into a flurry of standing up, reaching up, and getting situated in the aisle.

The mother in front of me smiled. "Congratulations," she said. "Sounds like you have it figured out more than most people."

The line began to move. "Not really. We just had a lot of hard lessons early on."

"Lucky you," she said, guiding her son down the aisle.

I laughed once, thinking about all the fuckups and let-downs, but she was right. If I had to do it all over again,

I'd rather endure the pain in the beginning than have had it easy and then have it all go to shit later on.

Shepley and I rushed to baggage claim, got our luggage, and then hurried outside to catch a cab. I was surprised to see a man in a black suit holding a dry erase board with MADDOX PARTY scribbled in red marker.

"Hey," I said.

"Mistah Maddox?" he said, smiling wide.

"That's us."

"I'm Mistah Gumbs. Right this way." He took my larger bag and led us outside to a black Cadillac Escalade. "You're staying at the Ritz-Carlton, yeah?"

"Yes," Shepley said.

We loaded the trunk with the rest of the bags, and then sat in the middle row of seats.

"Score," Shepley said, looking around.

The driver took off, buzzing up and down hills, and around curves, all on the wrong side of the road. It was confusing, because the wheel was on the same side as ours.

"Glad we didn't rent a car," I said.

"Yes, the majority of accidents here are caused by tourists."

"I bet," Shepley said.

"It's not hard. Just remember you are closest to the curb," he said, karate-chopping the air with his left hand.

He continued giving us a minitour, pointing out different things along the way. The palm trees made me feel enough out of our element, but the cars parked on the left side of the road were really messing with my head. Large hills seemed to touch the sky, peppered with little white specks—what I assumed were hillside houses.

"That's Havensight Mall, there," Mr. Gumbs said. "Where all the cruise ships dock, see?"

I saw the big ships, but I couldn't stop staring at the water. I'd never seen water such a pure blue before. I guess that's why they call it Caribbean blue. It was fucking unbelievable. "How close are we?"

"Gettin' there," Mr. Gumbs said with a happy grin.

Right on cue, the Cadillac slowed to a stop to wait for oncoming traffic, and then we pulled into a long drive. He slowed once more for a security booth, we were waved in, and then we continued on another long drive to the entrance of the hotel.

"Thanks!" Shepley said. He tipped the driver, and then pulled out his cell phone, quickly tapping on the screen. His phone made a kiss noise—must have been America. He read the message and then nodded. "Looks like you and I go to Mare's room, and they're getting ready in yours."

I made a face. "That's . . . odd."

"I guess they don't want you to see Abby, yet."

I shook my head and smiled. "She was that way last time."

A hotel employee showed us to a golf cart, and then he drove us to our building. We followed him to the correct room, and then we walked inside. It was very . . . tropical, fancy Ritz-Carlton tropical.

"This'll do!" Shepley said, all smiles.

I frowned. "The ceremony is in two hours. I have to wait two hours?"

Shepley held up a finger, tapped on his phone, and then looked up. "Nope. You can see her when she's ready. Per Abby. Apparently she misses you, too."

A wide grin spread across my face. I couldn't help it. Abby had that effect on me, eighteen months ago, a year ago, now, and for the rest of my life. I pulled out my cell phone.

Love you, baby.

OMG! You're here! Love u 2!

See u soon.

You bet ur ass.

I laughed out loud. I'd said before that Abby was my everything. For the last 365 days straight, she'd proved that to be true.

Someone pounded on the door, and I walked over to open it.

Trent's face lit up. "Asshat!"

I laughed once, shook my head, and motioned for my brothers to come in. "Get in here, you fuckin' heathens. I've got a wife waiting, and a tux with my name on it."

CHAPTER FIFTEEN

Happily Ever After

Travis

A year to the day after I stood at the end of an aisle in Vegas, I found myself waiting for Abby again, this time in a gazebo overlooking the rich blue waters surrounding St. Thomas. I pulled at my bow tie, pleased that I had been smart enough not to wear one last time, but I also didn't have to deal with America's "vision" last time.

White chairs with orange and purple ribbons tied around their backs sat empty on one side, the ocean sat on the other. White fabric lined the aisle Abby would walk down, and orange and purple flowers were pretty much everywhere I looked. They did a nice job. I still preferred our first wedding, but this looked more like what any girl would dream of.

And then, what any boy would dream of stepped out from behind a row of trees and bushes. Abby stood alone, empty-handed, a long, white veil streaming from her half-up, half-down hair, blowing in the warm Caribbean breeze. Her long, white dress was form fitting and a little shiny. Probably satin. I wasn't sure and I didn't care. All I could focus on was her.

I jumped the four steps that led up to the gazebo and jogged to my wife, meeting her at the back row of chairs.

"Oh my God! I've missed you like hell!" I said, wrapping her in my arms.

Abby's fingers pressed into my back. It was the best thing I'd felt in three days, since I'd hugged her good-bye.

Abby didn't speak, she just giggled nervously, but I could tell she was happy to see me, too. The last year had been so different from the first six months of our relationship. She had totally committed to me, and I had totally committed to being the man she deserved. It was better, and life was good. The first six months, I kept waiting for something bad to happen that would rip her away from me, but after that we settled into our new life.

"You are amazingly beautiful," I said after pulling back to get a better look.

Abby reached to touch my lapel. "You're not so bad yourself, Mr. Maddox."

After a few kisses, hugs, and stories about our bachelor/bachelorette parties (which seemed to be equally uneventful—except for the whole Trent stripper thing), the guests began to trickle in.

"Guess that means we should get in our places," Abby said. I couldn't hide my disappointment. I didn't want to be without her for another second. Abby touched my jaw and then rose up on her feet to kiss my cheek. "See you in a bit."

She walked off, disappearing behind the trees again.

I returned to the gazebo, and before long the chairs were all filled. We actually had an audience this time. Pam sat on the bride's side in the first row, with her sister and brother-in-law. A handful of my Sigma Tau brothers lined the back row, with my dad's old partner and his wife and kids, my boss Chuck and his girlfriend of the week, both sets of America's grandparents, and my Uncle Jack and Aunt Deana. My dad sat in the first row of the groom's side, keeping my brothers' dates company. Shepley stood as my best man, and my groomsmen, Thomas, Taylor, Tyler, and Trent, stood next to him.

We'd all seen another year pass, we'd all been through so much, in some cases lost so much, and yet come together as a family to celebrate something that had gone right for the Maddoxes. I smiled and nodded at the men standing with me. They were still the impenetrable fortress I remembered from my childhood.

My eyes focused on trees in the distance as I waited for my wife. Any second now she would step out and everyone could see what I saw a year before, and find themselves in awe, just like I was.

Abby

After a long embrace, Mark smiled down at me. "You are beautiful. I'm so proud of you, sweetheart."

"Thank you for giving me away," I said, a little embarrassed. Thinking about everything he and Pam had done for me made hot tears pool in my eyes. I blinked them away before they had a chance to spill down my cheeks.

Mark pecked my forehead. "We're blessed to have you in our lives, kiddo."

The music began, prompting Mark to offer his arm. I took it, and we walked down a small, uneven sidewalk that was lined with thick, flowering trees. America was worried it would rain, but the sky was nearly clear, and sun was pouring down.

Mark guided me to the end of the trees, and then we rounded the corner, standing just behind Kara, Harmony, Cami, and America. All of them but America were dressed in purple, strapless satin minidresses. My best friend wore orange. They were all absolutely beautiful.

Kara offered a small smile. "I guess the beautiful disaster turned into a beautiful wedding."

"Miracles do happen," I said, remembering the conversation she and I had what seemed like a lifetime ago.

Kara laughed once, nodded, and then gripped her small bouquet in both hands. She rounded the corner, disappearing behind the trees. Soon after Harmony, and then Cami, followed.

America turned, hooking her arm around my neck. "I love you!" she said with a squeeze.

Mark tightened his grip, and I did the same with my bouquet.

"Here we go, kiddo."

We rounded the corner, and the pastor motioned for everyone to stand. I saw the faces of my friends and new family, but it wasn't until I saw the wet cheeks of Jim Maddox that my breath caught. I struggled to keep it together.

Travis reached out for me. Mark held his hands over ours. I felt so safe in that moment, held by two of the best men I knew.

"Who gives this woman away?" the pastor asked.

"Her mother and I." The words stunned me. Mark had been practicing *Pam and I* all week. After hearing that, there was no holding back my tears as they welled up and spilled over.

Mark kissed my cheek, walked away, and I stood there with my husband. It was the first time I'd seen him in a tux. He was clean-shaven, and had recently gotten his hair cut. Travis Maddox was the kind of gorgeous every girl dreamed about, and he was my reality.

Travis tenderly wiped my cheeks, and then we stepped onto the platform of the gazebo, directly in front of the pastor.

"We are gathered here today to celebrate a renewal of vows . . ." the pastor began. His voice melted into the sounds of the ocean breaking against the rocks in the background.

Travis leaned in, squeezing my hand as he whispered, "Happy anniversary, Pidge."

I looked into his eyes, as full of love and hope as they were the year before. "One down, forever to go," I whispered back.

red hill

JAMIE McGUIRE

Read on for an exclusive extract

Prologue

Scarlet

THE WARNING WAS SHORT—SAID ALMOST IN PASSING. "The cadavers were herded and destroyed." The radio hosts then made a few jokes, and that was the end of it. It took me a moment to process what the newswoman had said through the speakers of my Suburban: *Finally*. A scientist in Zurich had *finally* succeeded in creating something that—until then— had only been fictional. For years, against every code of ethics known to science, Elias Klein had tried and failed to reanimate a corpse. Once a leader amid the most intelligent in the world, he was now a laughing stock. But on that day, he would have been a criminal, if he weren't already dead.

At the time, I was watching my girls arguing in the backseat through the rearview mirror, and the two words that should have changed everything barely registered. Two words, had I not been reminding Halle to give her field trip permission slip to her teacher, would have made me drive away from the curb with my foot grinding the gas pedal to the floorboard.

Cadavers. Herded.

Instead, I was focused on saying for the third time that the girls' father, Andrew, would be picking them up from school that day. They would then drive an hour away to Anderson, the town we used to call home, and listen to Governor Bellmon speak to Andrew's fellow firefighters while the local paper took pictures. Andrew thought it would be fun for the girls, and I agreed with him—maybe for the first time since we divorced.

Although most times Andrew lacked sensitivity, he was a man of duty. He took our daughters, Jenna, who was just barely thirteen and far too beautiful (but equally dorky) for her own good, and Halle, who was seven, bowling, out to dinner, and the occasional movie, but it was only because he felt he should. To Andrew, spending time with his children was part of a job, but not one he enjoyed.

As Halle grabbed my head and jerked my face around to force sweet kisses on my cheeks, I pushed up her thick, black-rimmed glasses. Not savoring the moment, not realizing that so many things happening that day would create the perfect storm for separating us. Halle half jogged, half skipped down the walkway to the school entrance, singing loudly. She was the only human I knew who could be intolerably obnoxious and endearing at the same time.

A few speckles of water spattered on the windshield, and I leaned forward to get a better look at the cloud cover overhead. I should have sent Halle with an umbrella. Her light jacket wouldn't stand up to the early spring rain.

The next stop was the middle school. Jenna was absently discussing a reading assignment while texting the most recent boy of interest. I reminded her again as we pulled into the drop-off line that her father would pick her up at the regular spot, right after he picked up Halle.

"I heard you the first ten times," Jenna said, her voice slightly deeper than average for a girl her age. She looked at me with hollow brown eyes. She was present in body, but rarely in mind. Jenna had a wild imagination that was oh-so-random in the most wonderful way, but lately I couldn't get her to pay attention to anything other than her cell phone. I brought her into this world at just twenty. We practically grew up together, and I worried about her, if I'd done everything—or anything—right; but somehow she was turning out better than anyone could have imagined anyway.

"That was only the fourth time. Since you heard me, what did I say?"

Jenna sighed, peering down at her phone, expressionless. "Dad is picking us up. Regular spot."

"And be nice to the girlfriend. He said you were rude last time."

Jenna looked up at me. "That was the old girlfriend. I haven't been rude to the new one."

I frowned. "He just told me that a couple of weeks ago."

Jenna made a face. We didn't always have to say aloud what we were thinking, and I knew she was thinking the same thing I wanted to say, but wouldn't.

Andrew was a slut.

I sighed and turned to face forward, gripping the steering wheel so tightly my knuckles turned white. It somehow helped me to keep my mouth shut. I had made a promise to my children, silently, when I signed the divorce papers two years before: I would never bad-mouth Andrew to them. Even if he deserved it . . . and he often did.

"Love you," I said, watching Jenna push open the door with her shoulder. "See you Sunday evening."

"Yep," Jenna said.

"And don't slam the . . ."

A loud bang shook the Suburban as Jenna shoved the door closed.

". . . door." I sighed, and pulled away from the curb.

I took Maine Street to the hospital where I worked, still gripping the steering wheel tight and trying not to curse Andrew with every thought. Did he have to introduce every woman he slept with more than once to our daughters? I'd asked him, begged him, yelled at him not to, but that would be inconvenient, not letting his girl-of-the-week share weekends with his children. Never mind he had Monday through Friday with whoever. The kicker was that if the woman had children to distract Jenna and Halle, Andrew would use that opportunity to "talk" with her in the bedroom.

My blood boiled. Dutiful or not, he was an asshole when I was married to him, and an even bigger asshole now.

I whipped the Suburban into the last decent parking spot in the employee parking lot, hearing sirens as an ambulance pulled into the emergency drive and parked in the ambulance bay.

The rain began to pour. A groan escaped my lips, watching coworkers run inside, their scrubs soaked from just a short dash across the street to the side entrance. I was half a block away.

TGIF.

TGIF.

TGIF.

Just before I turned off the ignition, another report came over the radio, something about an epidemic in Europe. Looking back, everyone knew then what was going on, but it had been a running joke for so long that no one wanted to believe it was really happening. With all the television shows, comics, books, and movies about the undead, it shouldn't have been a surprise that somebody was finally both smart and crazy enough to try and make it a reality.

I know the world ended on a Friday. It was the last day I saw my children.

Chapter One

Scarlet

MY CHEST HEAVED AS THE THICK METAL DOOR CLOSED loudly behind me. I held out my arms to each side, letting water drip off my fingertips onto the white tile floor. My once royal-blue scrubs were now navy, heavily saturated with cold rainwater.

A squashing sound came from my sneakers when I took a step. *Ick*. Not much was worse than wet clothes and shoes, and it felt like I'd jumped into a swimming pool fully dressed. Even my panties were wet. We were only a few days into spring, and a cold front had come through. The rain felt like flying death spikes of ice.

Flying death spikes. *Snort*. Jenna's dramatic way of describing things was obviously rubbing off on me.

I slid my name badge through the card reader and waited until the small light at the top turned green and a high-pitched beep sounded, accompanied by the loud click of the lock release. I had to use all of my body weight to pull open the heavy door, and then I stepped into the main hallway.

Fellow coworkers flashed me understanding smiles that helped to relieve some of my humiliation. It was obvious who all had just arrived on shift, about the time the sky opened up and pissed on us.

Two steps at a time, I climbed the stairs to the surgical floor and snuck into the women's locker room, stripping down and changing into a pair of light-blue surgery scrubs. I held my sneakers under the hand dryer, but only for a few seconds. The other X-ray techs were waiting for me downstairs. We had an upper GI/small bowel follow-through at 8:00, and this week's radiologist was more than just a little grumpy when we made him run behind.

Sneakers still squishing, I rushed down the steps and back down the main hallway to Radiology, passing the ER double doors on my way. Chase, the security guard, waved at me as I passed.

"Hey, Scarlet," he said with a small, shy smile.

I only nodded, more concerned with getting the upper GI ready on time than with chitchat.

"You should talk to him," Christy said. She nodded in Chase's direction as I breezed by her and her piles of long, yellow ringlets.

I shook my head, walking into the exam room. The familiar sound of my feet sticking to the floor began an equally familiar beat. Whatever they cleaned the floor with was supposed to sanitize the worst bacteria known to man, but it left behind a sticky residue. Maybe to remind us it was there—or that the floor needed to be mopped again. I pulled bottles of barium contrast from the upper cabinet, and filled the remaining space with water. I replaced the cap, and then shook the bottle to mix the powder and water into a disgusting, slimy paste that smelled of bananas. "Don't start. I've already told you no. He looks fifteen."

"He's twenty-seven, and don't be a shrew. He's cute, and he's dying for you to talk to him."

Her mischievous smile was infuriatingly contagious. "He's a kid," I said. "Go get the patient."

Christy smiled and left the room, and I made a mental note of everything I'd set on the table for Dr. Hayes. God, he was cranky; particularly on Mondays, and even more so during shitty weather.

I was lucky enough to be somewhat on his good side. As a student, I had cleaned houses for the radiologists. It earned me decent money, and was perfect since I was in school forty hours a week at that time. The docs were hard asses in the hospital, but they helped me out more than anyone else while I was going through the divorce, letting me bring the girls to work, and giving me a little extra at Christmas and on birthdays.

Dr. Hayes paid me well to drive to his escape from the city, Red Hill Ranch, an hour and a half away in the middle-of-nowhere Kansas to clean his old farmhouse. It was a long drive, but it served its purpose: No cell service. No Internet. No traffic. No neighbors.

Finding the place on my own took a few tries until Halle made up a song with the directions. I could hear her tiny voice in my head, singing loudly and sweetly out the window.

West on Highway 11
On our way to heaven
North on Highway 123
123? 123!

Cross the border
That's an order!
Left at the white tower
So Mom can clean the doctor's shower
Left at the cemetery
Creepy . . . and scary!
First right!
That's right!
Red! Hill! Rooooooooad!

After that, we could make it there, rain or shine. I'd even mentioned a few times that it would be the perfect hideaway in case of an apocalypse. Jenna and I were sort of post-apocalyptic junkies, always watching end-of-the-world marathons and preparation television shows. We never canned chicken or built an underground tank in the woods, but it was entertaining to see the lengths other people went to.

Dr. Hayes's ranch would make the safest place to survive. The cupboards and pantry were always stocked with food, and the basement would make any gun enthusiast proud. The gentle hills kept the farmhouse somewhat inconspicuous, and wheat fields bordered three sides. The road was about fifty yards from the north side of the house, and on the other side of the red dirt was another wheat field. Other than the large maple tree in the back, visibility was excellent. Good for watching sunsets, bad for anyone trying to sneak in undetected.

Christy opened the door and waited for the patient to enter. The young woman stepped just inside the door, thin, her eyes sunken and tired. She looked at least twenty pounds underweight.

"This is Dana Marks, date of birth twelve, nine, eighty-nine. Agreed?" Christy asked, turning to Dana.

Dana nodded, the thin skin on her neck stretching over her tendons as she did so. Her skin was a sickly gray, highlighting the purple under her eyes.

Christy handed the woman loose folds of thin blue fabric. "Just take this gown behind the curtain there, and undress down to your underpants. They don't have any rhinestones or anything, do they?"

Dana shook her head, seeming slightly amused, and then slowly made her way behind the curtain.

Christy picked up a film and walked to the X-ray table in the middle of the room, sliding it into the Bucky tray between the table surface and the controls. "You should at least say hi."

"Hi."

"Not me, dummy. To Chase."

"Are we still talking about him?"

Christy rolled her eyes. "Yes. He's cute, has a good job, has never been married, no kids. Did I mention cute? All that dark hair . . . and his eyes!"

"They're brown. Go ahead. I dare you to play up brown."

"They're not just brown. They're like a golden honey brown. You better jump on that now before you miss your chance. Do you know how many single women in this hospital are salivating over that?"

"I'm not worried about it."

Christy smiled and shook her head, and then her expression changed once her pager went off. She pulled it from her waistline and glanced down. "Crap. I have to move the C-arm from OR 2 for Dr. Pollard's case. Hey, I might have to leave a little early to take Kate to the orthodontist. Do you think you could do my three o'clock surgery? It's easy peasy."

"What is it?"

"Just a port. Basically C-arm babysitting."

The C-arm, named for its shape, showed the doctors where they were in the body in real time. Because the machine emitted radiation, it was our jobs as X-ray techs to stand there, push, pull, and push the button during surgery. That, and make sure the doctor didn't over-radiate the patient. I didn't mind running it, but the damn thing was heavy. Christy would have done the same for me, though, so I nodded. "Sure. Just give me the pager before you leave."

Christy grabbed a lead apron, and then left me to go upstairs. "You're awesome. I wrote Dana's history on the requisition sheet. See you later! Get Chase's number!"

Dana walked slowly from the bathroom, and I gestured for her to sit in a chair beside the table.

"Did your doctor explain this procedure to you?"

Dana shook her head. "Not really."

A few choice words crossed my mind. How a doctor could send a patient in for a procedure without an explanation was beyond me, and how a patient couldn't ask wasn't something I understood, either.

"I'll take a few X-rays of your abdomen, and then fetch the doctor. I'll come back, make the table vertical, and you'll stand and drink that cup of barium," I said, pointing to the cup behind me on the counter, "a sip at a time, at the doctor's discretion. He'll use fluoroscopy to watch the barium travel down your esophagus and into your stomach. Fluoro is basically an X-ray, but instead of a picture, we get a video in real time. When that's done, we'll start the small bowel follow-through. You'll drink the rest of the barium, and we'll take X-rays as it flows through your small bowel."

Dana eyed the cup. "Does it taste bad? I've been vomiting a lot. I can't keep anything down."

The requisition page with Christy's scribbles was lying on the counter next to the empty cups. I picked it up, looking for the answer to my next question. Dana had only been ill for two days. I glanced up at her, noting her appearance.

"Have you been sick like this before?" She shook her head in answer. "Traveled recently?" She shook her head again. "Any history of Crohn's disease? Anorexia? Bulimia?" I asked.

She held out her arm, palm up. There was a perfect bite mark in the middle of her forearm. Each tooth had broken the skin. Deep, red perforations dotted her arm in mirrored half-moons, but the bruised skin around the bites was still intact.

I met her eyes. "Dog?"

"A drunk," she said with a weak laugh. "I was at a party Tuesday night. We had just left, and some asshole wandering around outside just grabbed my arm and took a bite. He might have pulled a whole chunk off if my boyfriend hadn't hit him. Knocked him out long enough for us to find the car and leave. I saw on the news yesterday that he'd attacked other people, too. It was the same night, and the same apartment complex. Had to be him." She let her arm fall to her side, seeming exhausted. "Joey's in the waiting room . . . scared to death I have rabies. He just got back from his last tour in Afghanistan. He's seen everything, but he can't stand to hear me throw up." She laughed quietly to herself.

I offered a comforting smile. "Sounds like a keeper. Just hop up on the table there, and lay on your back."

Dana did as I asked, but needed assistance. Her bony hands were like ice.

"How much weight did you say you've lost?" I asked while situating her on the table, sure I had read Christy's history report wrong on the requisition.

Dana winced from the cold, hard table pressing against her pelvic bone and spine.

"Blanket?" I asked, already pulling the thick, white cotton from the warmer.

"Please." Dana hummed as I draped the blanket over her. "Thank you so much. I just can't seem to get warm."

"Abdominal pain?"

"Yes. A lot."

"Pounds lost?"

"Almost twenty."

"Since Tuesday?"

Dana raised her brows. "Believe me, I know. Especially since I was thin to begin with. You . . . don't think it's rabies . . . do you?" She tried to laugh off her remark, but I could hear the worry in her voice.

I smiled. "They don't send you in for an upper GI if they think it's rabies."

Dana sighed and looked at the ceiling. "Thank God."

Once I positioned Dana, centered the X-ray tube, and set my technique, I pressed the button and then took the film to the reader. My eyes were glued to the monitor, curious if she had a bowel obstruction, or if a foreign body was present.

"Whatcha got there, buddy?" David asked, standing behind me.

"Not sure. She's lost twenty pounds in two days."

"No way."

"Way."

"Poor kid," he said, genuine sympathy in his voice.

David watched with me as the image illuminated the screen. When Dana's abdomen film filled the screen, David and I both stared at it in shock.

David touched his fingers to his mouth. *"No way."*

I nodded slowly. "Way."

David shook his head. "I've never seen that. I mean, in a textbook, yes, but . . . man. Bad deal."

The image on the monitor was hypnotizing. I'd never seen someone present with that gas pattern, either. I couldn't even remember seeing it in a textbook.

"They've been talking a lot on the radio this morning about that virus in Germany. They say it's spreading all over. It looks like war on the television. People panicking in the streets. Scary stuff."

I frowned. "I heard that when I dropped off the girls this morning."

"You don't think the patient has it, do you? They're not really saying exactly what it is, but that," he said, gesturing to the monitor, "is impossible."

"You know as well as I do that we see new stuff all the time."

David stared at the image for a few seconds more, and then nodded, snapping out of his deep thought. "Hayes is ready when you are."

I grabbed a lead apron, slid my arms through the armholes, and then fastened the tie behind my back as I walked to the reading room to fetch Dr. Hayes.

As expected, he was sitting in his chair in front of his monitor in the dark, speaking quietly into his dictation mic. I waited patiently just outside the doorway for him to finish, and then he looked up at me.

"Dana Marks, twenty-three years old, presenting with abdominal pain and significant weight loss since Wednesday. Some hair loss. No history of abdominal disease or heart problems, no previous abdominal surgeries, no previous abdominal exams."

Dr. Hayes pulled up the image I'd just taken, and squinted his eyes for a moment. "How significant?"

"Nineteen pounds."

He looked only slightly impressed until the image appeared on the screen. He blanched. "Oh my God."

"I know."

"Where has she been?"

"She hasn't traveled recently, if that's what you mean. She did mention being attacked by a drunk after a party Tuesday night."

"This is profound. Do you see the ring of gas here?" he asked, pointing to the screen. His eyes brightened with recognition. "Portal venous gas. Look at the biliary tree outline. Remarkable." Dr. Hayes went from animated to somber in less than a second. "You don't see this very often, Scarlet. This patient isn't going to do well."

I swallowed back my heartbreak for Dana. She either had a severe infection or something else blocking or restricting the veins in her bowel. Her insides were basically dead and withering away. She might have four more days. They would probably attempt to take her to emergency surgery, but would likely just close her back up. "I know."

"Who's her doctor?"

"Vance."

"I'll call him. Cancel the UGI. She'll need a CT."

I nodded and then stood in the hall while Dr. Hayes spoke in a low voice, explaining his findings to Dr. Vance.

"All right. Let's get to it," the doctor said, standing from his chair. We both took a moment to separate ourselves from the grim future of the patient. Dr. Hayes followed me down the hall toward the exam room where Dana waited. "The girls doing okay?"

I nodded. "They're at their dad's this weekend. They're going to meet the governor."

"Oh," the doctor said, pretending to be impressed. He'd met the governor several times. "My girls are coming home this weekend, too."

I smiled, glad to hear it. Since Dr. Hayes's divorce, Miranda and Ashley didn't come home to visit nearly as much as he would have liked. They were both in college, both in serious relationships, and both mama's girls. Much to the doctor's dismay, any free time they had away from boyfriends and studying was usually spent with their mother.

He stopped, took a breath, held the exam-room door open, and then followed me inside. He hadn't given me time to set up the room before he came back, so I was glad the upper GI was cancelled.

David was shaking the bottles of barium.

"Thanks, David. We won't be needing those."

David nodded. Having seen the images before, he already knew why.

I helped Dana to a sitting position, and she stared at both of us, clearly wondering what was going on.

"Dana," Dr. Hayes began, "you say your problem began early Wednesday morning?"

"Yes," she said, her voice strained with increasing discomfort.

Dr. Hayes abruptly stopped, and then smiled at Dana, putting his hand on hers. "We're not going to do the upper GI today. Dr. Vance is going to schedule you a CT instead. We're going to have you get dressed and go back to the waiting room. They should be calling you before long. Do you have someone with you today?"

"Joey, my boyfriend."

"Good," the doctor said, patting her hand.

"Am I going to be okay?" she said, struggling to sit on her bony backside.

Dr. Hayes smiled in the way I imagined him smiling while speaking to his daughters. "We're going to take good care of you. Don't worry."

I helped Dana step to the floor. "Leave your gown on," I said, quickly grabbing another one and holding it behind her. "Slip this on behind you like a robe." She slipped her tiny arms through the holes, and then I helped her to the chair beside the cabinet. "Go ahead and put on your shoes. I'll be right back. Just try to relax."

"Yep," Dana said, trying to get comfortable.

I grabbed her requisition off the counter and followed the doctor to the workroom.

As soon as we were out of earshot, Dr. Hayes turned to me. "Try to talk to her some more. See if you can get something else out of her."

"I can try. All she mentioned out of the ordinary was the bite."

"You're sure it wasn't an animal?"

I shrugged. "She said it was some drunk guy. It looks infected."

Dr. Hayes looked at Dana's abnormal gas patterns on the monitor once more. "That's too bad. She seems like a sweet kid."

I nodded, somber. David and I traded glances, and then I took a breath, mentally preparing myself to carry such a heavy secret back into that room. Keeping her own death from her felt like a betrayal, even though we'd only just met.

My sneakers made a ripping noise as they pulled away from the floor. "Ready?" I asked with a bright smile.

Chapter Two

BY LUNCH, DANA HAD ALREADY BEEN IN AND OUT OF surgery. Christy told us they only opened her up long enough to see there was nothing they could do, before closing her back up. Now they were waiting for her to awaken so they could tell her she would never get better.

"Her boyfriend is still with her," Christy said. "Her parents are visiting relatives. They're not sure they'll get back in time."

"Oh, Jesus," I said, wincing. I couldn't imagine being away from either of my daughters in a situation like that, wondering if I would make it in time to see her alive one last time. I shook it off. Those of us in the medical field didn't have the luxury of thinking about our patients' personal lives. It became too close. Too real.

"Did you hear about that flu?" Christy said. "It's all over the news."

I shook my head. "I don't think it's a flu."

"They're saying it has to do with that scientist over in Europe. They say it's highly contagious."

"Who are *they*? *They* sound like troublemakers to me."

Christy smiled and rolled her eyes. "*They* also said it's breached our borders. California is reporting cases."

"Really?"

"That's what they say," she said. Her pager buzzed. "Damn, it's getting busy." She pushed a button and called upstairs, and then she was gone again.

Within the hour, the hospital was crowded and frantic. The ER was admitting patients at a hectic pace, keeping everyone in radiology busy. David called in another tech so he and I could cover the ER while everyone else attended to outpatients and inpatients.

Whatever it was, the whole town seemed to be going crazy. Car accidents, fights, and a fast-spreading virus had hit at the same time. On my sixth trip to the ER, I passed the radiology waiting room and saw a group of people crowded around the flat-screen television on the wall.

"David?" I said, signaling for him to join me in front of the waiting room. He looked in through the wall of glass, noting the only seated person was a man in a wheelchair.

"Yeah?"

"I have a bad feeling about this." I felt sick watching the updates on the screen. "They were talking about something like this on the radio this morning."

"Yeah. They were reporting the first cases here about half an hour ago."

I stared into his eyes. "I should leave to try to catch up to my girls. They're halfway to Anderson by now."

"As busy as we are, no way is Anita going to let you leave. Anyway, it's highly contagious, but disease control maintains that it's just a virus, Scarlet. I heard that those that got the flu shot are the ones affected."

That one sentence, even unsubstantiated, immediately set my mind at ease. I hadn't had a flu shot in three years because I always felt terrible afterward, and I'd never gotten one for the girls. Something about vaccinating for a virus that may or may not protect against whatever strain came through didn't sit well with me. We had enough shit in our bodies with hormones and chemicals in our foods and everyday pollutants. It didn't make sense to subject ourselves to more, even if the hospital encouraged it.

Just as David and I finished up our last batch of portable X-rays in the ER, Christy rounded the corner, looking worn.

"Has it been as busy down here as it's been up there?"

"Yes," David said. "Probably worse."

"Can you still do that port for me?" Christy said, her eyes begging.

I looked to David, and then back at Christy. "The way things are going, if I take that pager, I'll be stuck up there until quitting time. They really need me down here."

David looked at his watch. "Tasha comes in at three thirty. We can handle it until then."

"You sure?" I asked, slowly taking the pager from Christy.

David waved me away dismissively. "No problem. I'll take the pager from you when Tasha gets here so you can go home."

I clipped the pager to the waistband of my scrubs, and headed upstairs, waving good-bye to Christy.

She frowned, already feeling guilty. "Thank you very, very much!"

I passed Chase for the umpteenth time. As the hours

passed, he'd looked increasingly nervous. Everyone was. From the looks of things inside the ER, it seemed like all hell was breaking loose outside. I kept trying to sneak peeks at the television but once I finished one case, the pager would go off again to direct me to another.

Just as I had anticipated, once I arrived on the surgery floor, there would be no leaving until David relieved me at 3:30. Case after case, I was moving the C-arm from surgery suite to surgery suite, sometimes moving a second one in for whomever was called up for a surgery going on at the same time.

In one afternoon I saw a shattered femur, two broken arms, and a broken hip, and shared an elevator with a patient in a gurney accompanied by two nurses, all on their way to the roof. His veins were visibly dark through his skin, and he was covered in sweat. From what I could make of their nervous banter, the patient was being med-flighted out to amputate his hand.

My last case of the day was precarious at best, but I didn't want to have to call David up to relieve me. My girls were out of town with their father, and David had a pretty wife and two young sons to go home to. It didn't make sense for me to leave on time and for him to stay late, but I had already logged four hours of overtime for the week, and that was generally frowned upon by the brass.

I walked past the large woman in the gurney, looking nervous and upset. Her hand was bandaged, but a large area was saturated with blood. I remembered her from the ER, and wondered where her family was. They all had been with her downstairs.

Angie, the circulation nurse, swished by, situating her surgical cap. It was covered in rough sketches of hot-pink lipsticks and purses. As if to validate her choice of head cover, she pulled out a tube of lip gloss and swiped it across her lips. She smiled at me. "I hear Chase has been asking about you."

I looked down, instantly embarrassed. "Not you, too." Was everyone so bored that they had nothing better to do than fantasize about my non-love life? Was I that pathetic that a prospect for me was so exciting?

She winked at me as she passed. "Call him, or I'm going to steal him from you."

I smiled. "Promise?"

Angie rolled her eyes, but her expression immediately compressed. "Damn! Scarlet, I'm sorry, your mom is on line two."

"My mom?"

"They transferred her call up a couple of minutes before you came in."

I glanced at the phone, wondering what on earth she would be calling me at work about. We barely spoke at all, so it must have been important. Maybe about the girls. I nearly lunged for the phone.

"Hello?"

"Scarlet! Oh, thank God. Have you been watching the news?"

"A little. We've been slammed. From the few glimpses I've gotten, it looks bad. Did you see the reports of the panic at LAX? People were sick on some of the flights over. They think that's how it traveled here."

"I wouldn't worry too much about it. Nothing ever happens in the middle of the country."

"Why did you call, then?" I said, confused. "Are the girls okay?"

"The girls?" She made a noise with her throat. Even her

breath could be condescending. "Why would I be calling about the girls? My kitchen floor is pulling up in the corner by the refrigerator, and I was hoping you could ask Andrew to come fix it."

"He has the girls this weekend, Mother. I can't really talk right now. I'm in surgery."

"Yes, I know. Your life is so important."

I glanced at Angie, seeing that she and the surgical tech were nearly finished. "I'll ask him, but like I said, he has the girls."

"He has the girls a lot. Have you been going to the bars every weekend, or what?"

"No."

"So what else is more important than raising your children?"

"I have to go."

"Sensitive subject. You've never liked to be told you're doing something wrong."

"It's his weekend, Mother, like it is every other weekend."

"Well. Why does his weekend have to be the weekend I need help?"

"I really have to go."

"Did you at least send dresses with them so their daddy can take them to church? Since he's the only one who seems to care to teach them about the Lord."

"Good-bye, Mother." I hung up the phone and sighed just as Dr. Pollard came in.

"Afternoon, all. This shouldn't take long," he said. He held his hands in front of him, fingers pointing up, waiting for Angie to put gloves on them. "But by the looks of it we're all in for a long night, so I hope none of you had plans."

"Is that true?" Ally, the scrub ... mask. "About LAX?"

"It happened at Dulles, too," Angie ...

I glanced at the clock, and then ... from the front pocket of my scrubs. I co... someone felt like ratting me out for being ... piece of paper in my file was worth it in this ca... ...out the words *Call Me ASAP*, and then sent them ...o Jenna's phone.

After a couple of minutes with no response, I dialed Andrew. It rang four times, then his voicemail took over.

I sighed. "It's Scarlet. Please call me at the hospital. I'm in surgery, but call me anyway so we can coordinate. I'm coming there as soon as I get off work."

Nathan

ANOTHER EIGHT-HOUR DAY THAT DIDN'T MEAN A DAMN thing. When I clocked out from the office, freedom should have been at the forefront of my mind, or should have at least brought a smile to my face, but it didn't. Knowing I had just wasted another day of my life was depressing. Tragic, even. Stuck at a desk job for an electric co-op that made no difference in the world, day in and day out, and then going home to a wife who hated me made for a miserable existence.

Aubrey hadn't always been a mean bitch. When we first got married, she had a sense of humor, she couldn't wait until it was bedtime so we could lie together and kiss and touch. She would owjob because she wanted to please me, not because my birthday.

Seven years ago, she changed. We had Zoe, and my role switched from desirable, adoring husband to a source of constant disappointment. Aubrey's expectations of me were never met. If I tried to help, it was either too much, or it wasn't done the right way. If I tried to stay out of her way, I was a lazy bastard.

Aubrey quit her job to stay home with Zoe, so mine was the only source of income. Suddenly that wasn't enough, either. Because I didn't make what Aubrey felt was enough money, she expected me to give her a "baby break" the second I walked in the door. I wasn't allowed to talk to my wife. She would disappear into the den, sit at the computer, and talk to her Internet friends.

I'd entertain Zoe while emptying the dishwasher and prepping dinner. Asking for help was a sin, and interrupting the baby break just gave Aubrey one more reason to hate me, as if she didn't have enough already.

Once Zoe started kindergarten, I hoped it would get better, that Aubrey would start back to work, and she would feel like her old self again. But she just couldn't break free of her anger. She didn't seem to want to.

Zoe had just a few weeks left in second grade. I would pick her up from school, and we would both hope Aubrey would turn away from the computer just long enough to notice we were home.

On a good day, she would.

Today, though, she wouldn't. The Internet and radio had been abuzz since early morning with breaking news about an epidemic. A busy news day meant Aubrey's ass would be stationed firmly against the stained, faded blue fabric of her office chair. She would be talking about it with strangers in forums, with friends and distant family on social networks, and commenting on news websites. Theories. Debates. Somewhere along the way it had become a part of our marriage, and I had been edged out.

I waited in my eight-year-old sedan, first in a line of cars parked behind the elementary school. Zoe didn't like to be the last one picked up, so I made sure to go to her school right after work. Waiting forty minutes gave me enough time to decompress from work, and psych myself up for another busy night without help or acknowledgment from my wife.

The DJ's tone was more serious than it had been, so I turned up the volume. He was using a word I hadn't heard them use before: *pandemic*. The contagion had breached our shores. Panic had broken out in Dulles and LAX airports when passengers who'd fallen ill during their international flights began attacking the airline employees and paramedics helping them off the plane.

In the back of my head, I knew what was happening. The morning anchor had reported the arrest of a researcher somewhere in Europe, and while my thoughts kept returning to how impossible it was, I knew.

I looked into the rearview mirror, my appearance nearly unrecognizable to anyone that had known me in better days. The browns of my eyes were no longer bright and full of purpose like they once were. The skin beneath them was shaded with dark circles. Just fifteen years ago I was two hundred pounds of muscle and confidence; now I felt a little more broken down every day.

Aubrey and I met in high school. Back then she wanted to touch me and talk to me. Our story wasn't all that exciting: I was on the starting lineup of a small-town football team, and she was head cheerleader. We were both big fish in a small pond. My light-brown, shaggy hair moved when a breeze passed through the passenger side window. Aubrey used to love how long it was. Now all she did was bitch that I needed a haircut. Come to think of it, she bitched about everything when it came to me. I still went to the gym, and the women at work were at times a little forward, but Aubrey didn't see me anymore. I wasn't sure if it was being with her that sucked the life out of me, or the disappointments I'd suffered over the years. The further away I was from high school, the less making something of myself seemed possible.

An obnoxious buzzing noise on the radio caught my attention. I listened while a man's robotic voice came over the speakers of my car. "This is a red alert from the emergency broadcast system. Canton County sheriff's department reports a highly contagious virus arriving in our state has been confirmed. If at all possible, stay indoors. This is a red alert from the emergency broadcast system . . ."

Movement on the side of my rearview mirror caught my attention. A woman was sprinting from her car toward the door of the school. Another woman jumped from her minivan and, after a short pause, ran toward the school as well with her toddler in her arms.

They were mothers. Of course they wouldn't let the logical side of their brain talk them into hesitation. The world was going to hell, and they were going to get their children to safety . . . wherever that was.

I shoved the gearshift into park and opened my door. I walked quickly, but as frantic mothers ran past me, I broke into a run as well.

Inside the building, mothers were either carrying their children down the hall to the parking lot, or they were quickly pushing through the doors of their children's classrooms, not wasting time explaining to their teachers why they were leaving early.

I dodged frightened parents pulling their confused children along by the hand until I reached Zoe's classroom. The door cracked against the concrete wall as I yanked it open.

The children looked at me with wide eyes. None of them had been picked up yet.

"Mr. Oxford?" Mrs. Earl said. She was frozen in the center of her classroom, surrounded by mini desks and chairs, and mini people. They were patiently waiting for her to hand out the papers they were to take home. Papers that wouldn't matter a few hours from now.

"Sorry. I need Zoe." Zoe was staring at me, too, unaccustomed to people barging in. She looked so small, even in the miniature chair she sat in. Her light-brown hair was curled under just so, barely grazing her shoulders, just the way she liked it. The greens and browns of her irises were visible even half a classroom away. She looked so innocent and vulnerable sitting there; all the children did.

"Braden?" Melissa George burst through the door, nearly running me down. "Come on, baby," she said, holding her hand out to her son.

Braden glanced at Mrs. Earl, who nodded, and then the boy left his chair to join his mother. They left without a word.

"We have to go, too," I said, walking over to Zoe's desk.

"But my papers, Daddy."

"We'll get your papers later, honey."

Zoe leaned to the side, looking around me to her cubby. "My backpack."

I picked her up, trying to keep calm, wondering what the

world would look like outside the school, or if I would reach my car and feel like a fool.

"Mr. Oxford?" Mrs. Earl said again, this time meeting me at the door. She leaned into my ear, staring into my eyes at the same time. "What's going on?"

I looked around her classroom, to the watchful eyes of her young students. Pictures drawn clumsily in thick lines of crayon and bright educational posters hung haphazardly from the walls. The floor was littered with clippings from their artwork.

Every child in the room stared at me, waiting to hear why I'd decided to intrude. They would keep waiting. None of them could fathom the nightmare that awaited them just a few hours from now—if we had that much time—and I wasn't going to cause a panic.

"You need to get these kids home, Mrs. Earl. You need to get them to their parents, and then you need to run."

I didn't wait for her reaction. Instead I bolted down the congested hallway. A traffic jam seemed to be causing a bottleneck at the main exit, so I pushed a side door to the pre-K playground open with my shoulder, and with Zoe in my arms, hopped the fence.

"Daddy! You're not supposed to climb the fence!"

"I'm sorry, honey. Daddy's in a hurry. We have to pick up Mommy and . . ."

My words trailed off as I fastened Zoe into her seatbelt. I had no idea where we would go. Where could we hide from something like this?

"Can we go to the gas station and get a slushie?"

"Not today, baby," I said, kissing her forehead before slamming the door.

I tried not to run around the front. I tried, but the panic and adrenaline pushed me forward. The door slammed shut, and I tore out of the parking lot, unable to control the fear that if I slowed down even a little bit, something terrible would happen.

One hand on the steering wheel, and the other holding my cell phone to my ear, I drove home, ignoring traffic lights and speed limits and trying to be careful not to get nailed by other panicked drivers.

"Daddy!" Zoe yelled when I drove over a bump too fast. "What are you doing?"

"Sorry, Zoe. Daddy's in a hurry."

"Are we late?"

I wasn't sure how to answer that. "I hope not."

Zoe's expression signaled her disapproval. She always made an effort to parent Aubrey and me. Probably because Aubrey wasn't much of one, and it was clear on most days that I didn't know what the hell I was doing.

I pressed on the gas, trying to avoid the main roads home. Every time I tried to call Aubrey from my cell, I got a weird busy signal. I should have known when I got there that something was wrong. I should have immediately put the sedan in reverse and raced away, but the only thing going through my head was how I would convince Aubrey to leave her goddamned computer, what few things we would grab, and how much time I should allow to grab them. An errant thought ran through my head about how much time it would take the Internet to cease, and how ironic it was that a viral outbreak would save our marriage. There were so many *should haves* in that moment, but I ignored them all.

"Aubrey!" I yelled as I opened the door. The most logical

place to look was the den. The empty blue office chair was a surprise. So much so that I froze, staring at the space as if my vision would correct itself and she would eventually appear, her back to me, hunched over the desk while she moved just enough to maneuver the mouse.

"Where's Mommy?" Zoe asked, her voice sounding even smaller than usual.

A mixture of alarm and curiosity made me pause. Aubrey's ass had flowed over and cratered in the deteriorated cushion of that office chair for years. No noise in the kitchen, and the downstairs bathroom door was open, the room dark.

"Aubrey!" I yelled from the second step of the stairs, waiting for her to round the corner above me and descend each step more dramatically than the last. At any moment, she would breathe her signature sigh of annoyance and bitch at me for something—anything—but as I waited, it became obvious that she wouldn't.

"We're going to be very late," Zoe said, looking up at me.

I squeezed her hand, and then a white envelope in the middle of the dining table caught my eye. I pulled Zoe along with me, afraid to let her out of my sight for a second, and then picked up the envelope. It read "Nathan" on the front, in Aubrey's girly yet sloppy script.

"Are you serious?" I said, ripping open the envelope.

Nathan,

By the time you get this I'll be hours away. Your probably going to think I'm the most selfish person in the world, but being afraid of you thinking bad of me isn't enough for me to

stay. I'm unhappy and I've been unhappy for a
long time.

I love Zoe, but I'm not a mother. You are the
one that wanted to be a father. I knew you
would be a good daddy, and I thought that
you being a good daddy would make me a good
mother, but it didn't. I can't do this anymore.
There are so many things I want to do with my
life and being a housewife isn't one of them.

I'm sorry if you hate me, but I've finally
decided I can live with that. I'm sorry you have
to explain this to Zoe. I'll call tomorrow when
I'm settled and try to help her understand.

Aubrey

I let the folded paper fall to the table. She could never spell
you're correctly. That was just one of a hundred things about
Aubrey that bothered me but I never mentioned.

Zoe was looking up at me, waiting for me to explain or
react, but I could do neither. Aubrey had left us. I came back
for her lazy, cranky, miserable ass, and she fucking left us.

A scream outside startled Zoe enough for her to grip my
leg, and reality hit about the same time that bullets came crash-
ing through the kitchen windows. I ducked, and signaled Zoe
to duck with me.

There would be no calling Aubrey's friends and relatives to
find out where she was so I could beg her to come back. I had to
get my daughter to safety. Aubrey might have picked a horrible
first day for independence, but it was what she wanted, and I
had a little girl to protect.

More screams. Car horns honking. Gunfire. *Jesus. Jesus, Jesus, Jesus.* It was here.

I opened the hallway closet and grabbed my baseball bat, and then walked over to my daughter, kneeling in front of her to meet her tear-glazed eyes. "Zoe, we're going to have to get back to the car. I need you to hold my hand, and no matter what you see or hear, don't let go of my hand, do you understand?"

Zoe's eyes filled with more tears, but she nodded quickly.

"Good girl," I said, kissing her on the forehead.

Chapter Three

Scarlet

"BIT OFF?" THE NURSE, JOANNE, ASKED, CAREFULLY prepping the patient's hand. "By a dog?"

"I don't know," Ally said, her voice muffled behind her mask. She was a new hire for the scrub tech team, just out of school. She was twenty, but the way her big eyes were staring at the patient's hand made her look all of twelve. "Some kind of animal."

"Her son," I said, waiting with my X-ray equipment for the surgeon to arrive. Joanne and Ally looked at the meaty, exposed knuckle. "I took the X-rays," I added. "She was pretty shaken, but she said her son bit off her thumb."

Angie walked through the door with tiny steps. Her scrub pants made a swishing sound as she busily finished different tasks around the room.

"Are you sure she said her son?" Ally asked, staring at the site of the missing digit with renewed interest.

"He's in the ER," Angie said. "I heard he's exhibiting signs of rabies. Several people are."

"You don't think this has anything to do with what's been on the news, do you?" Ally asked, nervous. "Could it have made it here already from Germany? Could it spread that fast?"

The room grew quiet then.

The anesthesiologist had been nervous from the beginning about putting Margaret Sisney under. Instead of playing on his cell phone like usual, he stood over her, focused on every rise of her chest. He looked away every few seconds to focus on the numbers on the monitor, and then returned his attention to Margaret. It was hard to tell with the rest of her under blue surgical sheets, but her face and neck were visibly bluish in color. "She's cyanotic," he explained. He adjusted several knobs, and then prepared a syringe.

"Dr. Ingram," the nurse said to the anesthesiologist. "The patient's fingernails."

Even through the orange-brown tint of the iodine scrub, Margaret's nails were blackening.

"Shit," Dr. Ingram said. His eyes bounced back and forth between the patient and the monitor. "This was a mistake. A big damn mistake!"

Margaret's thumb was on ice across the room, waiting to be reattached. It was cyanotic as well, and Dr. Ferber's call to take her to surgery when she wasn't quite stable in the ER was questionable, even to a newly graduated X-ray tech like me. I watched as her stats deteriorated, and moved my equipment to the far wall, knowing a Code Blue was imminent.

My pager vibrated against my skin, and I reached under my top to grab it from the waistline of my scrubs. "Shit. Angie, I've got to set up in OR Four, and then I'm off. I'll send David up here. He'll have the pager."

"It's probably going to be a while, anyway, if we do it at all," Angie said, opening packages and buzzing around the room.

I rushed to the end of the hall, pushing and pulling heavy X-ray equipment in front of and behind me. The moment I finished setting up for the next patient, the call came over the intercom system.

"Code Blue. OR Seven. Code Blue. OR Seven," a woman's voice droned, sounding calm and apathetic.

I picked up the phone that hung on the wall by the door, and called down to the department. "Hey, it's Scarlet. I set up OR Four, but looks like Seven's going to be a while, if at all. Tell David to meet me at the south elevator on one. He needs to work this code, and I need to give him the pager."

As I walked down the hall, nurses, doctors, and anesthesiologists rushed past me, making their way to Margaret Sisney. I pushed the button for the elevator, and yanked the surgical mask off my face. When the doors opened, I sighed at the sight of the crowd inside.

"We've got room, Scarlet," Lana from accounting said.

"I'll uh . . . I'll take the stairs," I said, pointing with a small gesture to my right.

I turned on my heels, pushed through the double doors of the OR, and then used my shoulder to help offset the weight of the heavy door that led to the stairwell.

"One, two, three, four, five, six . . . ," I counted quickly, jogging down one set, and then the other. When I pushed my way into the hallway of the first floor, David was already waiting at the elevator.

"Enjoy," I said, tossing him the pager.

"Thanks, buddy. Have a good one," he said.

The crowd I'd left behind in the elevator exited, walking as a unit down the hall, in tight formation, their voices low and nervous as they discussed the latest news on the outbreak.

"Code Gray. ER One. Code Gray. ER One," a woman said over the intercom system.

Anita, the radiology manager, stood in the middle of the radiology hall with her arms crossed. Within moments, men from maintenance and from every other department scurried through the open double doors of the emergency room.

"What does Code Gray mean, rookie?" Anita asked with a smirk.

"Er . . . hostile patient?" I said, half guessing.

"Good!" she said, patting me on the back. "We don't hear those very often."

"Code Gray. ER Six. Code Gray. ER Six," the woman's voice called over the intercom. Her voice was less indifferent this time.

Anita looked down the hall of our department. "Something's not right," she said, her voice low. Julian, the CT tech, stepped out into the hallway. Anita waved him to the emergency room. "Go on!"

Julian obeyed, the ever-present bored expression momentarily absent from his face. As he passed, Anita gestured to the women's locker room. "You better clock out before I change my mind."

"You don't have to tell me twice." The keypad beeped after I pushed in the code, and then a click sounded, signaling me to enter. I walked in, noticing I was alone. Normally the room was abuzz with women opening their lockers, pulling out their purses, laughing and chatting, or cursing about their day.

As I spun my combination lock to access my locker, another announcement came over the intercom.

"Code Blue, ER Three. Code Blue, ER Three. Code Gray in the ambulance bay. Code Gray in the ambulance bay."

I grabbed my purse and slammed the door, quickly making my way down the hall. The radiology waiting room was on my way, separated from the hall with a wall of glass. The few patients inside were still focused on the flat screen. A news anchor was reporting with a scowl, and a blinking warning scrolled across the bottom of the screen. Most of the words were too small to make out, but I could see one: PANDEMIC.

A sick feeling came over me, and I walked quickly, on the verge of breaking into a sprint for the employee exit. Just as I opened the door, I heard a scream, and then more. Women and men. I didn't look back.

Running across the intersection to my Suburban in the southwestern lot, I could hear tires squealing to a stop. A nurse from the third floor was fleeing the hospital in a panic. She was afraid, and wasn't paying attention to the traffic. The first car barely missed her, but a truck barreled around the corner and clipped her body with its front right side. The nurse was thrown forward, and her limp body rolled to the curb.

My training urged me to go to her and check for a pulse, but something inside of me refused to let my feet move anywhere but in the direction of the parking lot.

Angie, the circulation nurse from upstairs, appeared in the doorway of the employee exit. Her surgery scrubs were covered from neck to knees in blood, her eyes wide. She was more cautious, dodging the traffic as she crossed.

"Oh my God, is that Shelly?" Angie asked. She rushed to

the curb and crouched beside the woman lying lifeless. Angie placed her fingers on the nurse's neck, and then looked up at me, eyes wide. "She's dead."

I wasn't sure what expression was on my face, but Angie jerked her head forward to insist I respond. "Did you see who hit her?" she asked.

"I don't think it's going to matter," I said, taking a step back.

Angie stood, and looked around. A police cruiser raced toward downtown. Other employees of the hospital began to filter out of the door, racing to the parking lot.

"I can't believe this is happening," she whispered, pulling her scrub hat from her short blond hair.

"Your scrubs," I said. A dark red streak ran down the front of her green standard-issue surgery scrubs. Her neck and cheek were also splattered with crimson.

"Mrs. Sisney flat-lined, and then woke up," Angie said, her face red and glistening with sweat. "She attacked Dr. Inman. I'm not sure what happened after that. I left."

I nodded and then backed away from her, toward the parking lot. Toward my Suburban. "Go home, Angie. Get your daughter and get the hell out of town."

She nodded in reply, and then looked down at the blood. "I should probably just go back in. I don't know how contagious this is. Kate's with my dad. He'll keep her safe."

Her eyes left her blood-saturated clothes and met mine. They were glossed over, and I could see that she had already given up. I wanted to tell her to try, but when the faces of my own children came to mind, my legs sprinted to the parking lot.

I threw my purse into the passenger seat and then inserted the key into the Suburban's ignition, trying to keep calm. It was

Friday, and my daughters were already an hour away, at their dad's for the weekend. Each possible route flashed in my mind. Scenes from post-apocalyptic movies with vehicles lining every lane of highways for miles did, too.

I pulled out my cell phone from my pocket and dialed Andrew's number. It rang, and rang, and rang, and then a busy signal buzzed in my ear instead of his voicemail. "It just started," I said quietly, putting my phone in the cup holder. "I can still get to them."

I tossed my phone into my purse, gripped the steering wheel with one hand, and shoved the gear into reverse with the other.

A part of me felt silly. The logical side of my brain wanted to believe I was overreacting, but there was no music on the radio. Only breaking news about the pandemic, the rising death toll, and the ensuing panic.

The Suburban stopped abruptly, and I turned around, seeing Lisa Barnes, the employee-health nurse, gripping her steering wheel, her eyes bulging. I'd backed up while she was pulling out of her parking spot, and we'd crashed into each other. I pushed open my door, and ran over to her.

"Are you okay?" I said, hearing the subdued panic in my voice.

"Get out of my fucking way!" she screamed as she gripped her gearshift and threw it into reverse.

Just then a pickup truck barreled through the lot and slammed into my Suburban, taking it all the way to the street.

Standing still beside Lisa's sedan in shock was the only thing I was capable of in that moment. My brain refused to process the surreal scene in front of me until I caught a glimpse of a crowd of people pushing through the side entrance, and fanning out into the street, joining others who were from other parts of town, running for their lives, too.

Drew Davidson, the human resources director, stumbled and fell. He cried out in pain, and then looked around him, reaching out to those passing by, screaming for help. No one so much as paused.

A pair of wild eyes stood out from the mob. It was Mrs. Sisney. She was moving quickly, into the dispersing crowd. She crossed the road and finally caught up to Drew, who was still on the ground, reaching for his ankle.

I watched in horror as Mrs. Sisney charged Drew, leaping on top of him and grabbing at his expensive suit while opening her mouth wide. Drew was pushing back against her, but she was a large woman, and eventually her body weight helped to press Drew's arms down enough for her to take a bite of his shoulder.

Drew's cries attracted someone else—whom I recognized as Mrs. Sisney's son—and another woman in scrubs. They ambled over to Drew's flailing legs and began to feed.

Lisa's screams matched Drew's, and then the crumpled front end of her sedan flew past me and toward the road as she left me standing in the parking lot to witness the horror alone.

A loud boom sounded in the distance. It was then that I noticed several pillars of smoke in the sky, the newest in the area of the blast. Gunshots added to the noise, both close and far away. The chaos was confusing and happening so fast I didn't have time to be afraid.

Shiny silver keys lay fanned out on the grass a few feet in front of Drew. He'd just bought a Jeep Wrangler the month before. I had only paid attention because I'd just lamented over

that Jeep in the showroom of the local Dodge dealership during lunch, and Drew had been sitting at our table. Not a week
later, when arriving for my shift, I saw that Jeep in the parking
lot, and Drew Davidson stepped out of it. He thanked me for
the tip, and that marked the first and last time he'd ever spoken
to me.

Taking even one step toward that scene was terrifying, but
I found enough courage to scoop up his keys and run for the
Jeep. My fingers pressed the keyless entry. I yanked the door
open, praying that the gas tank wasn't close to being empty.
Mrs. Sisney was still consuming the meat of Drew's neck and
the others were slowly gnawing on Drew's now lifeless body. *He
definitely wouldn't need his Jeep again*, I thought as I ripped out of
the parking lot.

Speed limits and red lights were irrelevant. I glanced from
one side to the other at each intersection, and then blew
through them until I reached the main road out of town. Surely
most people would head for the interstate, I thought, but I was
wrong. Wrecks peppered the old two-lane highway toward
Kellyville.

I kept the gas pedal pressed against the floorboard, trying
to stay away from traffic jams and buy myself some time to
think of what I should do. People, alive and dead, were running
around. Gunshots could be heard from all parts of town as
people shot reanimated corpses from their vehicles and porches.

A blinking sign signaled that I was entering a school zone.
My stomach instantly felt sick. The children had been picked
up more than an hour ago, thank God, but mine were so far
away. If the pandemic had spread so quickly, the girls were
probably terrified and running, too.

I had to get to them. My fingers tightened around the steering wheel. If it was the end of the world, I wanted to be holding my babies.

I turned up the volume on the radio, hoping for some clue about how to get out of town and to my children. Instead of reporting safety procedures or anything else helpful, the DJs were struggling to remain professional while one gruesome report after another came in about people being attacked, car accidents, and mayhem.

The one thing they weren't talking about was where the pandemic had originated. If either of the coasts had been struck first, it would have given me more time . . . and time was the only chance I had.